Twenty-five Short Stories

Peter Honey

First Edition published 2021
by
2QT Limited (Publishing)
Settle,
North Yorkshire BD24 9RH
United Kingdom

Cover design by Charlotte Mouncey with illustration by Peter Honey

Printed in Great Britain by TJ Books Limited

A CIP catalogue record for this book is available from the British Library

ISBN - 978-1-914083-36-5

For Carol Ann, Tim, Katie, James and David.

Contents

Introduction

I have written these short stories with the best of motives: to have fun. Now I'm hoping you'll have fun reading them, thus turning my stories into a win-win.

For two years, including throughout troublesome 2020, I produced stories at the rate of one every calendar month (an ideal lockdown pastime!). My Windsor U3A writing group met each month (remotely through the bad times) and I felt obliged to produce something for them to review. They were very good at it too, always suggesting improvements, correcting my punctuation and spotting numerous typos — a peer review group *par excellence*! Big thanks to Linda Ciardiello, Joy Smith and Astrid Thompson. Any mistakes that have escaped your scrutiny are my fault, not yours.

Thanks too for the encouragement provided by visitors to my website. Comments have always supportive and encouraging. One month when I was late with a story, three regular readers even emailed me separately to ask when the next story would appear and to check that I was okay. What it is to have an adoring public!

I've had a close encounter with short story writing before when I wrote *50 Cautionary Tales for Managers*, a paperback published in 2006. However, those stories were about real managers, people I'd met and worked with over the years. Despite my best efforts to disguise their identities, some managers still recognised themselves (and, amusingly, some were convinced they were in the book even though they weren't!). I run no such risks with the people in these stories because none of them exist: I made them up.

I have found writing short stories an intriguing process. Crafting them suits my short attention span (none exceed 3,000 words and most are less than 2,000 words) and I love the way they always seem to assume a life of their own. I just dream up a character and start writing, with no preconceived idea of where we'll finish up. It's akin to following a meandering river rather than getting from A to B on a motorway. Even when, often on one of my daily walks, an ending occurs to me, the story still insists on taking a circuitous route. See what I mean about having fun?

I tend to fiddle with my stories, making numerous tiny adjustments (I blame the 'cut and paste' facility on my laptop!). During the fiddling phase, my long-suffering wife, Carol, often asks me what I'm doing, naturally assuming I'm busy doing something worthwhile. Sheepishly, I have to admit that I am tinkering with my latest story.

My problem is that I don't really know how to decide when a story is finished. Apparently I'm not alone. When I've asked professional writers and artists how they decide when to stop, I've never received any convincing replies. 'That's an interesting question' most say, which is tantamount to saying

'I haven't a clue'.

Ah well, finished or not, I hope you enjoy reading my short stories.

Peter Honey, November 2021

The Artist

To give him his due, Algernon was the first to admit that he was an arrogant sod. An only son born into a wealthy family, brought up in a stately home with a flag flying from the tower, schooled by a private tutor, waited on by servants – he had led a charmed life.

When he was ten years old he had inherited an endowment from his grandfather who was accidentally shot by his gamekeeper. The inheritance was generous and obviated the need for Algernon to earn his living. Aged eighteen, he embarked on a round-the-world adventure, lingering in Thailand for three years and living a carefree existence as a beach bum, his beard and long hair bleached by the tropical sun. Despite an unashamed reputation for being selfish and promiscuous, his wealth and his Harley-Davidson, a throbbing armchair on wheels, were magnets for a constant stream of girlfriends.

He fancied himself as an artist and cultivated a style remarkably reminiscent of Gauguin. He was prolific, producing numerous colourful landscapes and portraits of his girlfriends in various stages of undress, and despatching batches of canvases back home where they were stored in the ballroom.

However, his carefree life came to an abrupt halt when his alcoholic father died from liver failure and his mother implored him to return home and take up his duties as the local squire. So, with a heavy heart, he sold the Harley-Davidson, bade his distraught girlfriends farewell and returned to Hertfordshire to find a forlorn flag still flying at half-mast.

Having studied the household accounts, he calculated that the current rate of expenditure, plus restoring crumbling stone-work and fixing a leaky roof, meant destitution within five years. So Algernon, energetic and still bronzed from his sojourn in the Far East, astonished his mother with an ambitious plan to turn the stately home and its 120-acre estate into a viable business. Never given to self-doubt, he negotiated a substantial loan from Coutts, the family's bankers for over one hundred years.

Algernon's entrepreneurial zeal knew no bounds. The lake was stocked and fishing rights sold. Glamping sites were built in the extensive woods, with a dozen luxury tree houses each accommodating up to six people and, for those with no head for heights, yurts strategically placed to ensure privacy. Areas were set aside for a whole variety of outdoor events: pop festivals, operas, hot-air balloons, vintage-car rallies, sculpture exhibitions. An undulating quad-bike track snaked its way round the extremities of the estate. A vineyard was established on a south-facing slope. Plans were in hand to create a golf course and a zip-wire adventure.

Algernon's mother was relocated to a restored cottage on the estate, and a wing of the main house was refurbished and set aside as a conference centre. The extensive outbuildings were converted into separate business units with a gin distillery, a pottery school, a jewellery maker and a weaver in residence. The large tithe barn was converted into an art gallery; Algernon's paintings looked splendid in pools of light provided by strategically placed spot lights.

The various activities, inside and out, were set up as separate profit centres, each with a manager incentivised to break even within three years and make handsome profits thereafter.

Algernon, feeling self-satisfied, adopted the habit of doing daily walkabouts, inspecting this and that, and urging staff on to greater heights. One day, when he completed his rounds by calling into the gallery before lunch, the duty manager told him that a young woman had visited earlier and left her card.

'She admired your paintings and was keen to meet you, sir. Something about a business proposition.'

Algernon read the card: Virginia Burnes-Eastmacott, with an upmarket Chelsea address. Intrigued and, as always, keen to explore new opportunities, Algernon phoned the number on the card and invited Ms Burnes-Eastmacott to lunch.

On the appointed day, an attractive blonde arrived in an open-top silver Mercedes, the generous tyres crunching on the gravel. She chuckled as Algernon opened her door and, as she swung her legs out of the driver's seat, her split skirt gave Algernon a fleeting glimpse of her firm thighs.

'Thanks for agreeing to see me,' she said with a broad smile as she offered a well-manicured hand. 'Call me Virginia.'

Over lunch in the orangery, they exchanged small talk. Virginia was unashamedly flirtatious and enthused about Algernon's paintings and his entrepreneurial flair. Algernon, lapping up the flattery and feeling well-disposed towards this young woman, attempted to refill her wine glass. 'No thanks, I'm driving,' she said, her hand hovering protectively over her glass.

Algernon sighed and topped up his own glass. 'So let's get to the point. I understand you have a business proposition to put to me. I'm all ears.'

'I thought you'd never ask.' Virginia gave him a smouldering sidelong glance. 'I wondered if you've ever considered exhibiting works by other artists in your gallery.'

'There have been some approaches but I've always turned them down. To be honest,' Algernon smirked, 'the gallery is an ego-trip. Why invite competition?'

'Just as I thought.' Virginia paused, uncrossed her shapely legs and leaned back, her skirt riding up generously to expose three more inches of her thighs. 'Suppose I knew someone who'd be happy for you to pass off his paintings as your own. Might that be of interest?'

'Why the hell would anyone want to do that?'

'It's a long story.' Virginia's blonde hair fell forwards. 'Suppose,' she said, deftly tossing back her hair and looking straight into Algernon's eyes, 'I show you some of his stuff. If you like it, I'll tell you more. If you don't, that's the end of the matter.'

'All very mysterious.' Algernon sipped more of his wine, undressed Virginia slowly with his eyes and wondered why she looked faintly familiar. 'Fine. I'll take a look. Nothing ventured, nothing gained.'

A week later a white van drew up and Virginia, looking incongruously immaculate, stepped out. 'I've half a dozen canvases in here, but don't look yet. Could someone carry them into the orangery?'

Once the paintings, each about six feet square, had been propped up around the walls of the orangery, Virginia, giggling like a mischievous schoolgirl, produced a large handkerchief. Standing on tiptoe, her breasts brushing lightly against Algernon's back, she blindfolded him and led him by the hand into the orangery. She spun him round three times and, with a flourish, whipped off the blindfold.

Algernon blinked as his eyes adjusted to the light. He was totally unprepared for the riot of colour that confronted him. The canvases, confident and bold, were of undulating landscapes with huge trees and a dramatic use of light and shade. He sank into a nearby cane chair and gazed at them in wonder.

'Who did these?'

'I knew you'd like them. I just *knew*!' exclaimed Virginia excitedly.

Algernon, mesmerised by the paintings and in no doubt that they were accomplished works of art, repeated his question, 'But who did them?'

'He's a friend of a friend of mine and he can't sell his stuff because he is serving a long prison sentence. He's gay and unfortunately he killed his partner, stabbed him through the heart with a kitchen knife during a lover's tiff. He claimed it was self-defence but he was found guilty of murder and sentenced to twenty years.'

'And he wants me to sell his paintings in my gallery?'

'Yes. His flat is full of unsold canvases and he is still painting. The prison governor is a bit of an admirer and has allowed him to set up a studio in a corner of the bricklaying workshop.'

'But what's the deal? What does he want from each sale? I obviously have to consider the reputational risk of exhibiting the work of a convicted murderer.'

'Ah,' said Virginia conspiratorially, 'but no one would know. He wants you to sign the paintings and exhibit them as your own. All he wants is a flat rate of £3,000 for each painting you sell.'

Algernon shook his head in disbelief. 'Weird. I'll have to think about it.'

Over the next week, Algernon nipped into the orangery each day to gaze at the paintings and reassure himself that they were as good as he had initially judged them to be. The more he looked, the more certain he became that they were exceptional works of art. He showed them to his latest live-in girlfriend and, unnecessarily professing she was no connoisseur, she too enthused about the paintings.

Algernon phoned Virginia. 'I've decided to give it a go. I'll exhibit the canvases for a trial period, let's say for a couple of months, without disclosing the artist's identity and see if we get any takers.'

The paintings were moved from the orangery and hung in the gallery. The price tag for each was a speculative £10,000.

Within a few days there were two encouraging developments. Firstly, a dealer snapped up a couple of the paintings and, having doubled the price, sold them on to a wealthy firm of solicitors with plush headquarters in Canary Wharf. Miffed at losing out, Algernon immediately increased the asking price for each of the remaining canvases to £22,000.

Secondly, the gallery manager phoned Algernon to say that a reporter from the *Daily Telegraph* was in the gallery enquiring about the paintings. Was it convenient for Algernon to have a word with her?

The woman, introducing herself as Rebecca Blain, explained that she was a freelance arts correspondent. She'd been tipped off by the dealer who'd acquired the two canvases and, having seen the paintings for herself, wanted to write a feature about the artist for the *Telegraph* magazine.

'They are amazing!' she said, her eyes sparkling with enthusiasm as she gazed at the paintings. 'I understand you are the artist?'

'I'm so glad you like them,' said Algernon, with an ostensibly modest shrug of the shoulders. 'A bit of a departure for me. I'm experimenting with a new style.'

It was agreed that Rebecca would return in a few days with a photographer to interview Algernon. He phoned Virginia with news of the latest development. 'Wow, that's wonderful! Just the sort of publicity we need,' she cooed.

True to her word, Rebecca returned complete with a laptop, a small recording machine and a photographer who introduced herself as Jennifer. Both women were young and attractive. Rebecca wore a low-cut white blouse that gave Algernon tantalising glimpses of her cleavage as she leaned forward to set up the recorder on the coffee table between them.

Meanwhile, Jennifer, designer jeans stretching tightly over her shapely bum, fussed around with a camera slung around her neck. 'Don't mind me,' she chuckled provocatively as she rearranged a large vase of lilies and consulted her light meter.

Algernon, basking in all the attention, waxed lyrical about his life as a hitherto undiscovered artist. As he gave them a guided tour of his studio, both women admired and giggled suggestively at his paintings of nude girlfriends. They visited the gallery in the tithe barn where Algernon posed in front of the canvases, each now signed 'Alg'. Jennifer, balancing precariously on a stepladder, took numerous photographs as Algernon joked that surely one would suffice.

A month later, as promised, Rebecca's article appeared in the weekend *Telegraph* magazine. Virginia phoned to congratulate Algernon on the double-page spread, and the footfall in the gallery immediately doubled. Two more canvases were bought by a dealer who haggled over the price, albeit half-heartedly. The white van returned to deliver another batch of canvases from the mysterious artist; to Algernon's undisguised disappointment, it was driven by a burly male driver,

Algernon painted 'Alg' in the bottom right-hand corner of each painting and personally supervised their hanging in the gallery, giving them prime position by removing some of his own paintings. Then he sat back to await developments.

He didn't have to wait long. An email arrived from Virginia.

I realise this will come as a bit of a shock, but I'm writing to inform you that I intend to sue you for copyright infringement unless you pay me one million pounds.

You have committed a serious criminal offence by misleading the public and passing off my artworks as your own. Penalties, if convicted, are a prison sentence and an unlimited fine.

Please confirm your acceptance of my terms within 48hrs or I shall instruct a leading barrister specialising in copyright law.

This is non-negotiable and NOT a hoax.

Virginia

Algernon was aghast. He showed the email to his mother. 'That's dreadful, dear, but you've only got yourself to blame allowing yourself to be taken in by those silly girls.'

He phoned Virginia. 'Why?' he wailed, feeling mightily sorry for himself.

'Remember Samantha in Thailand? The one you ditched as soon as she became pregnant?'

'Samantha?'

'Yes. She's my twin sister and the money's for her.'

Suddenly, Algernon knew why Virginia had always seemed vaguely familiar.

The Aspen Tree

*B*are trees branch forlornly
    Blood vessels feed a dirty cottonwool sky
And smoky clouds are passing by.

Maggie read the words again then, after polishing her reading glasses on her apron, looked at the questions that followed:

1. What does 'branch forlornly' convey to you?

2. Why do you think the poet uses blood vessels as a metaphor for 'feeding' the sky?

3. What do the descriptions of the sky tell you about the weather?

4. Assume these are the opening lines of a poem. How would you complete it?

Maggie sighed and glanced at her teenage son, dyslexic and disorganised, busy ferreting in the fridge. 'What other home-work have you got?'

'Oh, only some maths. Easy-peasy. What's for supper?' Simon was always hungry.

Maggie read the English homework again. She knew Simon would struggle to make sense of it. He was brilliant at maths and anything to do with computers, but spelling and English language were not his strengths. The poem was unattributed but Maggie suspected that Miss Phillips, Simon's doe-eyed English teacher, had written it herself. She made no secret of her ambitions to become a published poet.

'When does it have to be handed in?'

'Monday.' Simon, having abandoned the fridge, was now helping himself to a large chunk of bread with lashings of raspberry jam.

'Well,' said Maggie, knowing she was wasting her breath, 'don't leave it until Sunday evening. Get it over and done with so that you can enjoy the weekend.' Simon always left his homework until the last moment, hoping against hopeless odds that the passage of time would somehow make it disappear.

The next day Maggie enjoyed her usual lie-in. It was her Saturday treat after working all week as a receptionist at one of the local GP practices. She had been a single mum for six years. Soon after Simon's ninth birthday, her partner, Simon's father, had upped and left without warning and without leaving any trace of his whereabouts.

By the time she got out of bed, Simon had helped himself to breakfast. Abandoning his cereal dish and an empty milk carton on the kitchen table, he had gone to play football in the park. After football he usually went to a friend's house to play computer games and rarely returned before supper time.

Maggie, still in her dressing gown, made herself a cup of

coffee and pottered about unhurriedly. She gazed out of her kitchen window. Her fenced-in garden consisted of a patch of grass, a shed with roofing felt that needed attention and a mature aspen tree. The tree was far too large for her small garden but she loved watching it change through the seasons: the soft new green of spring; the endless trembling of its leaves throughout the summer; the blaze of yellow in the autumn, and its skeletal branches in the winter.

One rainy afternoon with nothing better to do, she had Googled 'aspen tree' and was intrigued to discover that Jesus had been crucified on a cross made from aspen wood. The Celts believed the shimmering leaves meant the tree was busy communicating between this world and the next. For Maggie the tree took on a new significance; she now knew it was a very special tree, a magic tree.

Unfortunately the neighbour who owned the property beyond the tree, a detached Edwardian house with a large garden, viewed it quite differently. He had often put notes through her letterbox grumbling about its size and its over-hanging branches. The unfriendly notes, always signed 'Percy Wallace, JP', complained about the way the tree cast long shadows over his vegetable patch, coating it with fluffy, cotton-like seeds in the summer and masses of yellow leaves in the autumn.

Maggie always ignored his requests to have tree 'attended to', but eventually a note arrived demanding that the tree be felled to make way for a new fence. Apparently Mr Wallace had discovered that the tree was encroaching on his property, with half the trunk in his garden and not hers.

Maggie, distressed at the prospect of chainsaws and feeling sick as she imagined the ease with which they could slice through a tree-surgeon's thigh, had sought advice from a local councillor she knew through the surgery. Imploring her not to tell anyone, he had suggested she should apply for a Tree Preservation Order. Maggie had been delighted when an order was forthcoming but, predictably, an indignant Mr Wallace had immediately appealed for it to be revoked. However, despite all his pompous huffing and puffing, the order had been confirmed and the fence had to be constructed with a kink in it to accommodate the trespassing tree trunk.

During the intervening two years, the hostile notes from Mr Wallace had ceased, though he continued pointedly to ignore Maggie when she was in her garden and confiscate Simon's footballs whenever they went over the fence.

At teatime, after a lazy day, Maggie smelt smoke from a bonfire. Mr Wallace often had bonfires in the autumn but this one was particularly intrusive. She closed the kitchen window and hurried upstairs to Simon's bedroom, tripping over piles of discarded clothes to reach the window with a better view.

She could see Mr Wallace burning old timbers from what had once been a substantial greenhouse. As the flames licked greedily around the dry wood, a woman burst out of the house and ran down the garden, shouting and waving her arms. Maggie couldn't hear what she was saying but it was obvious that she was highly agitated. When she reached Mr Wallace, the woman pummelled his chest but he pushed her aside.

Maggie watched as the woman, tottered backwards, tripped over a pile of timbers and fell. She lay flat on the ground with her head in the bonfire. Mr Wallace hesitated momentarily then grabbed the woman's outstretched arms and pulled her clear of the flames. Her hair was on fire but Mr Wallace quickly extinguished the flames by smothering them with his bare hands. Together they staggered back to the house and disappeared inside.

Maggie stood there, hardly believing what she had seen. She felt helpless, incapable of deciding what she should do. Phone the police? Rush round to see if she could help? As she stood there, her heart pounding, she saw the flashing blue lights of an ambulance arrive in the road. Meanwhile, the unattended bonfire continued to burn enthusiastically.

Maggie took a deep breath and attempted to pull herself together. She was about to go downstairs to retrieve her mobile phone when a section of Mr Wallace's precious fence started to smoulder, suddenly igniting as if someone had doused it in petrol. The flames, like nimble squirrels, leapt up the branches of the aspen tree and its yellow leaves curled and writhed as they succumbed to the heat. At last Maggie sprang into action. She rushed downstairs and phoned 999.

The flames had died down by the time the fire engine arrived, leaving the aspen tree scorched and charred. Firemen, unable to reach the bonfire with their hoses, hacked a hole through the damaged fence and poured buckets of water over the dying embers. Steam hissed into the gathering dusk.

Maggie kept an eye on the Wallaces' house over the next few days, but it stayed dark with no signs of life. She wondered which hospital they'd been taken to, and imagined their burns swathed in soothing bandages. Meanwhile the leaves on the aspen tree that had escaped the flames fluttered ceaselessly. Maggie smiled to herself, confident they were busy relaying their story to the other world.

'What happened about your English homework?' Maggie

asked Simon the following weekend. 'Did you manage to complete that poem?'

'Yep,' said Simon, breaking open a packet of chocolate digestives.

'Let's have a look at what you wrote.'

Simon, half way through one of the biscuits, fished around in his rucksack and produced his English language exercise book. It had doodles all over the cover, including some sketches of Miss Phillips with exaggerated eyelashes.

Maggie turned the pages until she found the last entry. Simon had written:

My mum shouted, 'what the hell
That's next door's bonfire I can smell'.
A neighbour my mum can't stand
Allowed his bonfire to get out of hand.
Then, the daftest thing you ever heard,
The silly old fart set fire to his bird.
My mum's big tree caught fire too
Beyond the reach of the fire crew.
The branches now are black and bare
Looking much the worse for wear.

Maggie smiled. 'What did Miss Phillips say?'

'She said that I wasn't much of a poet but I certainly had a vivid imagination.'

The Class

I selected the course at random – literally. I picked up the prospectus from my local library and, before opening it, consulted a table of random numbers. It gave me 238: page twenty-three, line eight.

I delayed looking this up for a few hours, savouring the thrill of the unknown. Like Pooh relishing the moment before he began to eat honey, I love the anticipation.

Some of my best decisions have been arrived at randomly. I tossed a coin to decide which university to go to, which job offer to accept, which of two women I should ask to marry me, where to live, and so on. Even leaving my wife for another woman was decided on the roll of a dice.

Many years ago, I went on an enjoyable caravan holiday where our route was decided by the toss of a coin: heads turn right, tails turn left. By a circuitous route that took us through places I'd never have visited otherwise, and twice along lanes marked 'unsuitable for motor vehicles', we finished up on the outskirts of Leicester.

When eventually I turned to page twenty-three and counted

down to line eight. I found myself midway through a second paragraph extolling the virtues of an autobiographical writing course. Giving it no further thought (trust the numbers!), I enrolled and committed myself to twelve Wednesday mornings, 10am to 12.30pm.

The FE college was only a short walk from where I lived. A bored receptionist highlighted my name on her list and sent me up to Room Five on the third floor. I was the first to arrive. The room was anaemic: laminated tables in a U-shape; plastic chairs with splayed legs; a notice board by the door with a health and safety notice curling at the edges and another saying 'No food or drinks allowed in the classroom'; a clock on the wall, lopsided Venetian blinds on the widows; some spare chairs stacked in a corner, and a white board with ghostly marks from previous classes that hadn't quite been rubbed out.

Uninspiring. Short of terrorists bursting in with machine guns, it was hard to imagine how anything interesting could happen in such an innocuous room.

I sat down in what I judged to be the middle of the U-shape, placed my notebook in front of me like a dutiful schoolboy and waited. People arrived in dribs and drabs, mostly women, a couple of other men, twelve of us in total and all of a kind: all white and sixty-plus. We sat there self-consciously waiting for something to happen. I toyed with the idea of tossing a coin to see whether to stay or go, but I sat tight, curious to see where my random numbers had led me.

At exactly ten o'clock a slight woman, also in her sixties, with long grey hair that would have looked better gathered up in a bun and wearing a faded blue dress that reached down to her ankles, made her way to the front desk. Conversations petered out. She carried a ring binder, which she placed on the desk in front of her, and a handbag from which she produced a pair of spectacles.

This was Carolyn Gelling, our teacher.

She introduced herself in a quiet voice, telling us modestly that she was a published poet and author of some short stories that had been broadcast on Radio 4. She had been running the class twice yearly for the past five years.

'Of course,' she continued, 'we have strict rules about confidentiality.' For the first time she looked up, then hurriedly back down again as if surprised to find we were still there. 'For obvious reasons you must all agree never to divulge anything that is shared in this room. Confidentiality is essential.'

I wondered what the 'obvious reasons' could possibly be, but most people nodded compliantly.

Our teacher went on. 'I have your details from the enrolment forms you completed.' She paused and opened the ring-binder. 'But if you'd prefer anonymity, please feel free to adopt a pseudonym and I'll make a note of it.' She took a biro out of her handbag. 'All I ask is that you remember it. In my last group, some people forgot what they'd called themselves and blurted out their real names.' No trace of a smile.

She invited us to introduce ourselves and state briefly what we hoped to gain from the course. Everyone obliged and the introductions proceeded like a slow Mexican wave around the room in a clockwise direction. Most said they were happy to use their real names but four of us opted for anonymity, including me. I had surreptitiously tossed a coin and it told me to invent a name, so I chose John Boot after the character in Evelyn Waugh's satirical novel *Scoop*.

People had unremarkable expectations for the course; most just wanted to write about their lives to 'get it out of their system'. Two women, both enormously overweight, described themselves as 'damaged goods' and expressed the hope that putting pen to paper would be therapeutic. One of the men said he'd been a senior officer in the Met and had 'lots of stories to tell'. Another was a retired airline pilot who claimed to have been 'in a few scrapes'. A couple of people spoke vaguely about the possibility of getting their stuff published.

Apart from giving a false name, I told the truth: that I had chosen the course at random, but was open-minded and, never having done any writing previously other than formal reports, had no idea what to expect. Carolyn Gelling made no comment, though she looked at me over the top of her spectacles for a moment and I sensed that she thought my reasons for being there were inappropriately flippant.

We were briefed on the format for future sessions: each week four of us would be allocated a thirty-minute slot, ten minutes maximum to read aloud to the group followed by a twenty-minute critique. Carolyn assured us she'd keep a record and ensure that everyone had an equal number of turns.

She asked if anyone had brought something they'd written, otherwise she'd give us twenty minutes to write about anything we wished. Mercifully, two women came to the rescue and volunteered to read things that they had written. The first read a piece about the intricacies of making patchwork quilts, and the second – I found it hard to concentrate once I'd noticed red lipstick on her front teeth – about her summer holiday the year before in Malta.

And that was that. Our first session ended early and we all went our separate ways.

In preparation for the next class, I made a list of six possible topics I could write about and rolled a dice. The one that I hoped would win, about the joys of random decision making, was 'chosen'.

I wasn't allocated a slot at the next two meetings but I didn't care because, rather to my surprise, I found I was totally content listening to other people's stories. The youngest woman in the group, who was wearing a headscarf, read an account of an operation she'd undergone to remove a brain tumour. She'd been awake throughout so that she could give the surgeon a running commentary of what she could see and hear.

Another woman wrote about her schooldays at a convent where she had been sexually abused by a nun; she hadn't dared to tell anybody and, perhaps not surprisingly, had become a lapsed Catholic. The man from the Met told of a particularly tricky murder case he'd helped to investigate that remained unsolved. The airline pilot recounted how, having left his wife for an air hostess twenty years younger than himself, without warning she had upped and left him, leaving a curt farewell note propped up against a Toby Jug on his mantelpiece.

Another woman told an amusing story about how she had been a Freemans' agent back in the 1980s and found a couple of pages of hard porn bound into the lingerie section of the catalogue. She had telephoned head office to report her find, and they had immediately sent a courier to deliver flowers and collect the offending publication. Apparently Freemans printed a million copies of their catalogue in those days, but no other rogue copies ever turned up and no one could explain how porn got into hers.

I was perfectly content to listen to these stories. I loved the variety and marvelled at the quality of the writing. After each reading, Carolyn Gelling invited comments from the group and some, invariably guarded and complimentary, would be forthcoming. Then Carolyn would trot out few suggestions for improvement. She had some pet themes: an opening paragraph that captured the attention of the reader; not being afraid to describe feelings; using short sentences, and having ambiguous endings that left the reader wanting more.

All rather repetitious and humdrum.

By the fourth meeting, we had all settled into a familiar routine. Carolyn consulted her list and called out the names of the four of us who hadn't yet given a reading: three of the women and me.

One of the women, who said her name was Ruth, volunteered to go first. She wore dark glasses and had never spoken before. She was obviously nervous and started reading hesitantly.

'I left school when I was eighteen and went to university. In the 1950s less than four percent of people went on to further education, and very few of them were women. We were expected to become secretaries or nurses before getting married and having children. I was one of the fortunate few.'

She read quietly and I strained to hear the words. She looked frumpy and rather downtrodden, and I wondered whether a story with such an unpromising opening could turn into something interesting.

'During my second year, I started to go out with a man. I know it will seem strange but I was still very naive. I hadn't had a serious boyfriend before, and I was still a virgin. He – I'll call him George – was an amusing companion and I was flattered that he was attracted to me. He'd done National Service before coming to university so he was three years older than me. He was one of the few students with a car, and he'd often turn up unexpectedly and whisk me off on a trip somewhere.'

By now, I was paying rapt attention. It was uncanny; she might have been describing me. I did National Service before going to university and I had an old banger...

'His spontaneity was unnerving at first, but I slowly got used to it. He'd suddenly turn up, hold out two fists and say "Which one, left or right?". Then off we'd go to a steam rally or to a country pub or for an impromptu picnic. It was fun.'

My spine started to tingle. Was there something vaguely familiar about her voice, about the way she tilted her head?

'But he was unreliable, sometimes disappearing for a few weeks without any explanation. I began to worry that he might have another girlfriend but I was always glad when he turned up again, and he got tetchy if I questioned him. Then one day, without any warning, he told me that he couldn't go out with me anymore. He wouldn't say why, just something mysterious about not being in control of his own destiny.'

I gazed at the woman utter disbelief. Could this old woman possibly be the Sheila I'd known more than fifty years ago at university?

I took a coin out of my pocket: heads I scarpered, tails I stayed. Heads.

I got up, nodded apologetically to Carolyn and left. As I

closed the door quietly behind me, I heard Sheila continue. 'I was devastated. I didn't realise it at the time but he'd ruined my life.'

I never got to read my piece about the joys of random decision making.

The Collector

The room was sparsely furnished with just a table and four chairs. The only window was at ceiling height, and the fluorescent lights were unforgiving. Not a friendly room.

'Thank you for coming into the station, Dr Anderson. I am Detective Inspector Stuart Hinton and this is my colleague PC Ruth Palmer.' Like synchronised swimmers, they simultaneously proffered their IDs. Dr Anderson examined them carefully and eventually nodded. There was an obtrusive click as PC Palmer switched on the recorder.

'Could you please confirm your name and address?'

'Jeremy Anderson. 36 Holywell Street, Oxford.'

'I have to warn you that you are being interviewed under caution. You do not have to say anything, but it may harm your defence if you do not mention, when questioned, something you later rely on in court. Anything you say may be given in evidence.'

Dr Anderson nodded again. He was an earnest-looking young man, clean shaven with a neat parting in his hair. He was wearing spectacles, a sports jacket with two biros protruding from the top pocket, an open-neck shirt and jeans.

'I understand you have declined the offer of a solicitor.'

Another nod.

'You do appreciate that the services of a solicitor are free?'

Another nod.

'Well, it's for you to decide, but if you take my advice a solicitor should be present.'

'Why do I need a solicitor? I've done nothing wrong.'

'If you insist,' said the inspector. 'Could you tell us a little about yourself? Your occupation and marital status?'

Dr Anderson sighed, resigning himself to the inevitable questions. 'I'm single and I am employed as a post-doctoral researcher at the Pitt Rivers Museum in Parks Road. Could you tell me what this is about?'

'What is your area of research?'

'I'm an authority on tsantsas from Ecuador and Peru, and I'm heavily involved in the museum's labelling project.'

DI Hinton looked puzzled. 'For the record, what are tsantsas?'

Dr Anderson sighed again, seemingly exasperated at being confronted with such ignorance. He answered with exaggerated patience, as if addressing a class of primary-school children. 'They are shrunken heads made by the Shuar and Achuar people. They preserved the heads of their enemies to obtain the powers they believed were located in them. The concept of the tsantsa is that if someone does not die, then someone else cannot be born.'

The inspector and the constable exchanged glances as if to say 'we've got a right one here'. PC Palmer wrote 'shrunken heads' on her notepad and drew a circle around the words.

'And you say you are an authority on these shrunken heads?'

'Yes. I've visited Ecuador and Peru, and I'm in touch with other museums throughout the world with collections. I've had two academic papers published to date. It's a fascinating area of study.'

'Forgive me for asking, but have you ever been tempted to shrink a head yourself?' asked Inspector Hinton with a smirk.

'Very droll. Mind you,' added Dr Anderson, 'if I happened to come across a spare human head I'd know exactly what to do. First, I'd peel back the skin and hair and remove the bones, brain and other matter. Then I'd sew up the eye sockets and the mouth, pour sand into the cavity and soak the head briefly in hot water. The soaking process has to be repeated several times and, after each soaking, I'd shape the facial features. The resulting shrunken head would eventually finish up the size of a large orange.'

'You make it sound remarkably like a recipe.'

'Yes, my reading on the subject has been extensive,' said Dr Anderson proudly.

'And what is the labelling project?' asked DI Hinton.

'Well, if you'd visited the museum you'd know that most of the items on display have handwritten labels, some dating back to the 1880s. Unfortunately many of the labels, whilst they have a historical value, are no longer considered to be politically correct since they often contain words that are now considered to be derogatory or offensive. We are undertaking a big project to review the descriptions on the labels and decide whether they should be updated.'

'I see. So I take it that, in addition to shrunken heads, you have a particular interest in labels?'

'Yes. The director was delighted when I volunteered for the LMP.'

'LMP?'

'The Labels Matter Project.'

'Ah yes, of course.' PC Palmer wrote 'labels matter' on her pad followed by a large exclamation mark.

'What else can you tell us about labels?'

'The labels in the museum or labels in general?'

'Let's start with labels in general.'

Dr Anderson looked agitated. He avoided looking directly at the inspector and instead fixed his gaze on PC Palmer, not at her face but more at her neck. To her annoyance, Ruth Palmer felt herself blushing.

'May I ask what all this is about?' Dr Anderson asked again. 'Surely I have a right to know? After all, I'm attending this interview voluntarily.'

'Dr Anderson,' said Inspector Hinton patiently. 'We appreciate that you are here voluntarily but I urge you to cooperate with our enquiries. Please tell us more about your interest in labels.'

'You mean my collection?'

'You have a *collection*?'

'Yes,' said Dr Anderson. 'I have amassed a considerable collection, possibly the largest collection of clothing labels ever assembled.'

'Clothing labels? You have a collection of *clothing labels*?' asked DI Hinton, leaning forward and looking incredulous.

'Yes, a few hundred. They are all catalogued and filed by country of origin.'

'And where, may I ask, do the labels come from?'

'From all over the world. That's what's so fascinating. It's rather like stamp collecting.' Dr Anderson's eyes shone with excitement. 'Though I'll admit there is a preponderance of labels from China and Bangladesh. But lots in my collection are from countries such as Vietnam, India, Indonesia and the Philippines. Ethiopia and Morocco, too.'

'Forgive me. I meant where do *you* get the labels from, not where did they originate.'

'Oh sorry. Well, charity shops are a splendid source. I search the racks of clothing in the women's section looking for interesting labels to add to my collection. I used to buy the clothes and cut the labels off when I got home, but nowadays I carry a small pair of scissors with me and remove the labels in the shop.'

'Let me be clear. You remove the labels *in the shop?*'

'Yes. Though I say it myself, I've got it down to a fine art. I can snip a label off in a trice and slip it into my pocket.' Dr Anderson sat back, smiling happily, seemingly unaware that he could be incriminating himself.

Warming to his topic, he leaned forward again and added, 'I once succeeded in removing the label from the coat of a woman sitting immediately in front of me in the theatre. A coat made in Mexico, rather rare. She never felt a thing.'

The inspector and constable exchanged meaningful glances again. PC Palmer wrote the word 'scissors' on her notepad.

'Where else, aside from charity shops, do you acquire labels for your collection?'

'Shops on the high street are tempting but risky because it's difficult to dodge the security cameras. Pity,' added Dr Andrews wistfully, 'because many of the clothes in M&S are manufactured in places like Belgium, Austria and Germany. I could do with more labels from European countries to offset all those from the Far East.'

'Do you restrict your searches to woman's clothing?'

'Oh yes. Labels from women's garments are more varied. Most of the labels in my collection are from the back of the neck.' Dr Anderson looked directly at Constable Palmer. 'I wonder how many labels you have secreted about your person?'

Ruth Palmer squirmed with embarrassment.

Inspector Hinton held up his hand as if to say 'ignore that'. His tone was measured. 'Let me check that I've understood you correctly. You have amassed a collection of labels from women's clothing and have filed them according to the country where the garment was manufactured?'

Dr Anderson nodded.

'This is not an activity I have encountered before. What started your interest in clothing labels?'

Dr Anderson took a deep breath. 'It all started a few years ago at a concert I attended at the Holywell Music Rooms. Annoyingly, I was seriously distracted by the lady who sat in front of me. She had a label on her blouse that said "Size 18, made in China". She obviously didn't realise the label was sticking up behind her neck. I did my best to ignore it and concentrate on the music, but my eyes kept being drawn back to the label. I sat there wondering what, if anything, I could do. Eventually, after the interval when she returned to her seat, I leaned forward, tapped her on the shoulder and told her about the label. She was very embarrassed and tucked it away immediately. But even after the label was no longer on display, I couldn't stop thinking about what other labels she had inside her clothing.'

'I see. And have there been other occasions when you've noticed labels on unsuspecting women, sticking up or otherwise?'

'Oh yes. The very next day I was on a number three bus and a scantily clad young woman in front of me had a label on her black bra that could clearly be seen through her white top. I did my best to read what it said on the label, but the lettering was obscured by her blouse.'

'On this occasion the label was not sticking up?'

'No, it was attached to her bra. I was amazed that she thought it was okay to wear a black bra under a flimsy white top, but she had numerous studs in her ears and a ring through her nostril so I suppose she didn't really care.'

'Would you say you were attracted to this young woman?'

'Good Lord, no! My only interest was the label. Once I'd spotted it, I sat there wondering how many labels she had elsewhere and what they might say about countries of origin, and so on.'

'You weren't tempted to speak to her or follow her after she got off the bus?'

'Certainly not!' said Dr Anderson indignantly. 'In any case, I got off before her.'

Inspector Hinton said nothing. He just sat there looking directly at Dr Anderson, waiting for him to say more. Eventually, after an uncomfortably long silence, Dr Anderson added, 'Whenever I ask women if I may look at their labels, I do it politely and I'm careful to keep my scissors hidden.'

'Ah, so you admit you have been approaching young women?

We have received a number of complaints to that effect.'

'Complaints? There have been complaints?'

Inspector Hinton stood up abruptly. 'I'm terminating this interview forthwith.'

PC Palmer looked at her watch and spoke into the recording machine. 'The time is 11.23,' she said and clicked it off.

'Dr Anderson.' Inspector Hinton was already opening the door. 'We will resume this interview when you have a solicitor.'

'I've done nothing wrong. I don't need a solicitor.'

'Oh yes, you do,' said Inspector Hinton firmly as he left the room.

The Contest

The sandstone cliffs were increasingly unstable and large areas were cordoned off. Notices warned walkers to stay back from the edge and to keep dogs on leads. Beneath the cliffs there used to be a sandy stretch of beach, once popular with sunbathers and fossil hunters, but gradually it had disappeared under unsightly heaps of carboniferous limestone. The dark-grey boulders had been trucked in from quarries in the Mendip Hills and painstakingly placed on the beach by Dave and his yellow Caterpillar wheel loader.

Dave, or Sarge as he was known locally after a career in the Sappers serving in both Iraq and Afghanistan, was employed by the Environment Agency to carry out sea-defence work at Winkton-on-Sea.

He'd been lucky to land the job, a classic example of being in the right place at the right time. His mother lived in a hamlet along the coast from Winkton and, whilst staying with her after the unexpected death of his father, he had read in the local rag about the agency's plans to strengthen the sea defences. He immediately applied to join the team. After two interviews and some rigorous vetting, Dave had been highly chuffed when he was offered the job.

Winkton-on-Sea dated back to Saxon times. For many years it had suffered problems with coastal erosion, and during the last twenty years the pace of land loss had increased alarmingly. Large chunks of the grassy promenade had collapsed, a car park had been relocated and some buildings, including a gift shop, a pub and a small hotel, had surrendered to the elements, sliding gracelessly down a steep gradient of slippery clay.

The decision to import limestone boulders to create a barrier on the beach and construct four rock armour groynes had proved highly controversial and divided the local population. Fiercely opposed to the plan were the owners of a row of boarding houses and a café selling snacks and ice creams to holiday makers during the summer months. They feared that the loss of the sandy beach as an amenity would drastically reduce the number of visitors. Opposed also were the hapless owners of a colourful row of beach huts that the agency proposed to purchase compulsorily and bulldoze.

However, whilst the proposed loss of the beach was widely regretted, the majority of residents, most of them retired with properties that were likely to become uninsurable and worthless, were enthusiastic supporters of the intervention. So was a local entrepreneur who owned a golf club and a park of holiday chalets. The golf course had already had to be reconfigured after the sudden loss holes eight and nine and, as a precaution, some chalets had been taken apart and reassembled further from the cliff edge.

Dave had a vested interest in slowing the coastal erosion too, since his mother's bungalow, nearly a mile inland thirty years ago when his parents had first acquired it, was now only eighty yards from the unstable cliffs.

'Fancy you coming to the rescue like this,' remarked his mum, sipping a cup of tea. 'Dad would have been proud of you.'

'Yes,' said Dave, pulling on his boots. 'Limestone should definitely do the trick.'

Dave's task was to construct the rock groynes that jutted out to sea at right angles to the beach, and to connect them by placing piles of boulders on the sandy beach to prevent the waves undermining the unstable cliffs. Much of this work could only be done at low tide and when the sea was relatively calm.

A track was created so that fleets of lorries delivering the boulders could dump them close to the shoreline, and a brick building with stout metal doors was constructed to house Dave's yellow Caterpillar wheel loader and its huge hydraulic bucket.

Dave was a steady, conscientious worker, methodically plying back and forth in the loader for as long as the tides allowed. For much of the time he worked alone, perched high in the cab, scooping up boulders and bouncing on squishy tyres down the slope of the beach before releasing the boulders into what would become their watery grave.

Occasionally he would stop to exchange a few words with the lorry drivers, but otherwise he enjoyed the solitude, waving to the occasional passer-by and watching the seagulls wheeling inquisitively above his cab. Sometimes he'd have the radio on, but most times he just listened to the comforting throb of his diesel engine and, on sunny days with the cab doors flung open, to the endless swish-swashing of the sea.

Over the months, Dave developed a close affinity with the sea. He thought of it as his personal Goliath. He imagined that the waves exploring the rocks he had carefully placed in their path were alive and purposeful. On rough days, when the sea impeded his progress, he'd shake his fist and shout into the wind, 'Give us a break, Gol!' On calm days, with waves lapping lethargically around the wheels of the loader, Dave would thank the sea for its cooperation and give it a grateful thumbs up at the end of his shift. 'Thanks, mate. See you tomorrow.'

Inevitably the project suffered some setbacks. Sometimes the sea whipped itself up into a frenzy like a drunken, abusive partner, and reluctantly Dave would have to leave the loader in its garage and wait for it to sober up. Whilst his agency bosses fretted about delays and rising costs, he secretly admired the sea for putting up such a spirited show of resistance.

Once, an exceptional storm swept away one of the half-built groynes. On another occasion, the Caterpillar broke down and was stranded far out at low tide. In a race against the incoming waves, Dave eventually got the engine restarted but not before the swirling water was waist high.

'Bloody nearly got me there, mate,' Dave acknowledged, hauling himself up into the safety of his cab and giving the sea a respectful nod. 'Better luck next time, Goliath.'

Every month a group of managers from the agency would arrive, their white helmets and yellow jackets conspicuous against the dull grey of the limestone boulders. They'd stand in a group, their binoculars trained on the half-built groynes, then turn to inspect the crumbling cliffs.

'Nice job, Sarge,' said Dave's boss. 'You're definitely winning. Keep at it!'

'Will do, sir.' And off they'd go, leaving Dave to continue his battle against his Goliath.

Another occasional visitor was an elderly man who sat on a canvas stool watching the wheel loader coming and going. Dave had spotted him a number of times but had always been too far away to exchange words. One day the man appeared while Dave was sitting on a rock with his lunch box, eating the cheese-and-tomato sandwich his mum had prepared for him.

'Excuse me for intruding, but I've been admiring your handiwork. I'm a retired geologist with a special interest in coastal erosion.' The man smiled and proffered his hand. 'Ian North.'

Dave shook his hand. 'Pleased to meet you, sir. Dave Holmes. Everyone calls me Sarge.'

'Sarge for sergeant?'

'Yep, Sappers, twenty-five years.'

Dr North nodded, as if to say 'I thought as much'. 'An expensive investment, rock armour groynes. Do you know why the decision was made to use limestone rather than wood?'

'No, I came on board after the plans had been signed off. You'd need to contact the Environment Agency.'

'I might well do that. I don't like to interfere, but I wonder if they've estimated the likelihood of longshore drift.'

'Longshore drift? Beats me,' said Dave, brushing crumbs from his lap and taking a bite out of an apple. 'Best ask them.'

Dr North nodded again. 'It matters. Studies have demonstrated how TGS alters the natural flow of sediments and can dramatically increase coastal erosion on neighbouring beaches.'

'TGS? Afraid you've lost me.'

'Sorry, terminal groyne syndrome.' Dr North fixed his gaze accusingly on the left-hand groyne. 'It's a classic case of unintended consequences. You solve the problem in one area only to export it to another.'

'Must admit, that doesn't sound good, especially as I live just along the coast from here.'

'Best check it out,' said Dr North, folding up his stool.

That evening Dave Googled 'terminal groyne syndrome' and read:

Although groynes have a positive impact in reducing erosion, the areas on either side of the groynes can suffer from an even greater rate of erosion. The process of longshore drift transports materials away from neighbouring beaches and the groynes prevent replenishment. This allows the sea to reach the base of cliffs, even during neap tides, thus increasing rates of erosion and slumping.

Not wishing to alarm his mother, Dave chose to say nothing. At the weekend he did a recce, lacing up his boots and walking the length of the beach immediately below his mother's bungalow. Nothing had changed. He had a good look at the sandstone cliffs and could see no tell-tale cracks or signs of recent movement.

Back home, he carefully checked the grassy slope between his mother's garden fence and the cliff edge. Nothing untoward; it all looked fine. However, he decided to raise the matter with his boss on his next routine site visit.

'Who's been scaremongering? Minimal risk, old chap, minimal,' said his boss dismissively.

'But has the likelihood of longshore drift been taken into account? I need to know. I live about eighty yards back from the cliffs just east of here.'

'Sarge, I can assure you you've nothing to worry about. Nothing at all.'

'Well, sir, better safe than sorry. I'd like permission to extend the protection to the beaches on either side of the groynes.'

'Sorry, Sarge, but that's out of the question. We've already exceeded the £4.3million budgeted for this project. Afraid it's a definite no-no.'

But Dave remained wary and routinely checked the beach and the condition of the cliffs nearest to his mother's bungalow.

Then one day, after an autumn storm, there was no beach. It had gone. Vanished. The sea, like a giant vacuum cleaner, had sucked it up. Dave, balancing precariously on the nearest limestone groyne, rubbed his eyes in utter disbelief.

'Goliath, you sneaky bastard!' he shouted at the sea, now placid after the storm, its waves gently nibbling away at the base of the unprotected cliff.

He scrambled back over the rocks. Once he'd reached the track leading to the village that the lorries had trundled down over the past two years to deliver thousands of boulders, he stopped and turned to face the sea. Pulling himself up to his full height, he snapped his heels together and saluted.

Sounding remarkably like a sergeant major barking commands on a parade ground, he shrieked, 'Let's call it quits. You'll get the bungalow, but I've saved the village.'

Then he turned and marched home, wondering how to break the news to his mum.

The Demo

In a hotel in Derbyshire, a small group of amateur artists gather expectantly around Alison and Bob, two professionals. Outside, rain beats down horizontally.

Bob: Good morning all. This morning we are going to experiment. Alison and I are going work as a duo, putting marks down together to see what happens. It doesn't matter if we finish up with a mess – it's only a bit of paper, after all. We should probably be doing this outside where the wind and rain could play a legitimate part. *(Smiles to himself as he recalls other demos held outside in howling gales and driving rain, made possible by a see-through umbrella and the judicious use of bulldog clips.)*

Alison: *(Rolling up her sleeves and donning a large smock.)* Yes, even if we finish up looking silly, it isn't exactly life threatening. It's very important to overcome your inhibitions, to trust your intuition and see what happens.

Bob: *(Pouring copious amounts of water over a large sheet of white paper spread out on the table.)* Don't make the mistake of assuming that a painting should be descriptive or a narrative.

After all, you are just playing with the three main elements: LTC – line, tone and colour – another version of TLC. Ha ha, never thought of that before! You don't even need to use a brush. Your fingers will do, or a bit of old sponge, even a piece of stale bread. Turner often used bread, and he even kept one fingernail long so that he could scratch the surface of his canvas.

Alison: *(Selecting a large brush and plunging it into a blob of bright-pink watercolour.)* We'll work upside down – that's with the paper upside down, not us – partly so that you can see what we're doing but, more importantly, so that we don't get tempted to make anything resembling a representative image. *(Draws her brush across the paper leaving a large pink puddle in its wake.)* I love pink, definitely my favourite colour.

Bob: *(Producing a plate with copious amounts of green and blue paint squeezed out of tubes all around the rim.)* Oh Lord, I might have known it, much too much pink. Sorry, I shouldn't have said that. You can't have too much of *anything* – except pink, possibly. Nevertheless I feel the urge to retaliate with a lovely dark blue. *(Sweeps his brush clean through the middle of the pink puddle leaving a blue trail. A network of small tributaries spread out eagerly across the wet surface.)* That's better.

Alison: *(Dipping her brush into a bright yellow.)* Well, if I can't have pink, let's try my next favourite, a cheerful yellow. *(Makes a big yellow circle in the middle of the page.)* Of course, the paint would behave quite differently if we had the paper pegged out on a line.

Bob: Yes, it could even be a cylinder. You could have a large sheet of paper wrapped round an old oil drum and work your way round without ever being able to see the whole image.

Then you could release it, spread it out and see it for the first time. That's really exciting!

Alison: I once knew an artist who wore a large pair of thick specs whenever he painted so that everything was fuzzy and out of focus. Painting in a dark room would have the same effect.

Bob: Absolutely. *Anything* to intervene and change the relationship between the stereotypical way we have learnt to see things and the image on the page.

Alison: *(Warming to her task, splashes a lurid green across the bottom of the page.)* This is only schematic. I'm just laying it on. I want to capture the light, not to try to describe the actuality.

Bob: Ah, a rhythm is starting to happen here. (*Splashing on some turquoise.*) Suddenly, quite incongruously, we have little anomalies developing before our eyes. It's like being a magician pulling a rabbit out of a hat.

Alison: I wish you'd go easier with the blue. *(Applies more pink.)*

Bob: *(Enthusiastically.)* Oh, that's a lovely counterpoint tonally. Amazing subtlety! Watch the pink mingling with the blue. They have a wonderful resonance. I'm painting the sky and the water as if they are one.

Alison: Who said they were sky and water? I'm painting for the moment. We label things too easily. I want to get a general sense of place … to capture the wonder of a three-dimensional place in two dimensions with a nod towards composition.

Bob: We've got too many horizontals. We need something vertical and uplifting or diagonal and dramatic. *(Splashing a diagonal from the bottom left-hand corner of the page to the top right-hand corner.)* I have a sudden urge to cut this page in half. *(Seizes a pair of scissors.)*

Alison: Don't you dare! (*Folding the bottom third of the page under so that a vast area of green is no longer visible and applying more pink.*) I want this to have an ethereal quality.

Bob: Blast! I meant to take photos tracking the way the painting evolves. (*Whipping out a small camera and climbing on a chair to take a photo looking straight down at the page.*) You can learn a lot from deconstructing a painting and tracing its progression. Black-and-white photos are particularly helpful. Removing the distraction of colour reveals tonal qualities you'd otherwise miss.

Alison: Yes. I love the journey – the whole process – even more than the destination, a finished painting that, hopefully, will give someone pleasure.

Bob: There's never any need to feel apologetic. (*Holding up the paper so that the paint runs from top to bottom then, as the paint threatens to drip onto the floor, suddenly whipping the page back up so that the paint changes direction.*) Oh, this is fun! Let gravity do the work for us. Just look at the glorious accidental effects. You can always lift off some paint using the capillary action of the brush. (*Demonstrating, leaving pale areas wherever the tip of the brush comes into contact with the paper.*)

Alison: Well, I hope our little demonstration has shown you the importance of flouting convention. Rules are there to be broken.

Bob: Yes, we're using the language of paint to let go of our inhibitions. It's joyous to see where it takes you, not where you take it. (*Without warning, he puts a large blue streak across Alison's forehead.*) There, I've always wanted to do that!

Alison: Well, I did say it didn't matter if we finished up looking silly. (*Leaning over and dabbing bright pink on Bob's nose.*) Would anyone like to join in? Come on now, don't be shy, we can use any medium. Who said we were confined to a sheet of paper? Far too conventional.

The demo ends in disarray.

***

The phone on Alison's bedside table rings and she wakes with a start. She realises she has been dreaming.

Or has she? When she looks in the bathroom mirror, she can see traces of blue on her forehead.

The Dog Walker

It was only after we'd been meeting for a few months that it dawned on me that she never asked me any questions. None at all. Not a flicker of curiosity.

When we first met, on a crisp February morning with frost glistening on the fields, she'd chatted apologetically about her frisky new dog, explaining that he was only half way through his obedience training. By contrast, my rescue dog treated the enthusiastic sniffing and molesting with utter distain. I was proud of him.

On subsequent walks I learned about her husband – diabetic and grumpy; about her daughter – suffering from ME; about her son – unemployed and living at home again but drinking too much; about her mother – demented and living in a care home; about her house – in need of a new kitchen, and about her neighbours – noisy and unfriendly.

She told me her name, Glenda, and I told her mine, David, though I needn't have bothered because she never used it. I guessed she was in her late sixties, about my age. She was of average height, quite portly, with short hair dyed black. She wore a beret and 'sensible' clothes, and walked briskly in purposeful shoes with her head thrust forward. We always walked side by side, so eye contact between us was rare.

She greeted me cheerfully whenever we met and would immediately launch into updating me on the latest crises in her life: wisteria growing up the front of her house had dislodged the guttering; she was worried about her daughter being so lethargic; the car had failed its MOT but her husband didn't trust the garage; she'd visited her mother and noticed some bruises on her arms that the manager of the nursing home couldn't explain.

I always listened politely and said the occasional 'oh dear', but I found her one-way monologues increasingly tedious. After a while I started to vary the time of my morning walk in the hope of avoiding her. That would work well for a few days, sometimes even for a week or so, but no sooner was I back to relishing a solitary walk than she'd suddenly reappear. Had she lain in wait?

The outpourings would start all over again: her husband was having trouble with his feet and might have to have some toes amputated; it was her son-in-law's birthday and she was going to make a cake and take it round to her daughter's place; her son might be getting a job as a volunteer in a charity shop and he was going for an interview that very afternoon, if she could get him up in time; her bath was emptying slowly and she needed to get the plumber in to sort it out.

Not, alas, scintillating stuff. I considered my options.

Perhaps I should abandon my pre-breakfast walks or find somewhere else to walk the dog? But why the hell should I?

I wasn't sure I could cope with my dog's accusing looks if he was deprived of his early-morning scampers across the nearby fields. Anyway, I was addicted to starting my day by striding out whatever the weather, gulping fresh air, spotting the occasional deer, listening to the skylarks fluttering high in the skies above and, on my return journey, dropping into the newsagent to pick up my daily paper.

Perhaps I should level with Glenda and tell her that I preferred to walk alone, enjoying the seasons and mulling over this and that as I prepared myself for the day ahead. But she obviously loved what she called 'our little chats', and bumping into her from time to time was inevitable.

No, the answer was to set myself a challenge: to discover something *really fascinating* about her. Surely Glenda must have secrets, things she wasn't telling me or, better still, things she had never told anybody? For all I knew, she might be a spy or a pole dancer or an Olympic medallist.

So, I set to work digging and delving.

How many dogs had she had before this one? Three. What books did she enjoy? At present she was working her way through Mary Berry's *Simple Cakes*. Favourite television programme? Cooking programmes. Any hobbies, apart from baking cakes? Knitting. What music did she enjoy? Musicals, *South Pacific* was her favourite. What did she like doing most? Cooking and walking the dog. What was her favourite time of year? Spring. Did she drive? No, her husband did all the driving.

Glenda's answers were always forthcoming, even when I bombarded her with supplementary questions, but they still failed to convey anything that I considered fascinating.

I stepped up my efforts.

What was the worst thing that had ever happened to her? Falling off her bike and breaking her shoulder. The best thing? Having an extension put on the house. What would she do if she won the lottery? She didn't do the lottery, but if she did she'd invest any winnings in case she or her husband needed to pay for a nursing home. What was the naughtiest thing she had ever done? Pulled the arms off her sister's teddy bear. What was the best holiday she had ever had? The Canary Isles where she and her husband went for two weeks every year, always staying in the same hotel and meeting up with the same group of friends. And the worst? A week in Scarborough when it never stopped raining. Had she ever been really embarrassed? Yes, once in school assembly when the head teacher picked on her and asked her to stand up and spell Wednesday. She was flustered and forgot the 'd'. Everyone had laughed.

Try as I might, Glenda stayed doggedly beige. I decided to push my luck and try some more intrusive questions.

What do you dislike most about yourself? I wish I was taller and had longer legs. What's your biggest regret? My son not having a proper job. Have you ever been really drunk? No, alcohol doesn't agree with me. Have you ever cheated on your husband? What an odd question, certainly not! How many boyfriends did you have before you got married? None really. I met my husband when we were still at school.

All to no avail, my walking companion remained humdrum and dreary. Perhaps I should ask her where she bought her knickers? But I could guess the answer: M&S.

I decided to switch tactics and see if I could provoke

her into asking me a question, *any* question! Just for fun, I invented a scoring system: 1 for easy/banal questions such as 'Isn't it a nice day?'; 2 for personal questions such as 'Are you married?'; 3 for profound questions such as 'Do you believe in God?', and 4 for saucy questions such as 'How often do you have sex?'. My cunning plan was to let drop tantalising morsels of information about myself in the hope that sooner or later she'd take the bait.

On our next encounter, we discovered that the farmer had ploughed up the diagonal track we always took across a large field. Glenda was indignant. 'It's a right of way, he can't do that!'

'There's only one thing for it,' I said. 'Let's follow the old route and forge a new path.'

Cussedly, we set off, trudging across the deep furrows of newly turned soil. The going was heavy and Glenda, breathless and grumbling that she'd have to give her dog a bath, suddenly slipped and fell. Her unruly dog pranced round her prone body barking excitedly at the prospect of a new game.

Glenda stretched out her arms and, with some difficulty, I pulled her up. We'd never touched before and she said, 'Gosh, you're strong. My husband could never manage that.'

Seizing my opportunity I said, 'Yes, when I was younger I was a professional weight lifter, one of those guys in tight-fitting trunks with rippling muscles.'

'Oh dear,' she said looking down at the mud on her coat. 'What a mess.' Not a flicker of interest in my supposed career as a weight lifter. No curiosity about the muscles quivering beneath my clothing.

On another occasion, we met after I had been away on a

two-week family holiday in Minorca. As she approached, beaming happily, I felt sure she'd be curious about where I had been. Instead she said, 'Ah, there you are! I've been wanting to tell you about the gypsies who offered to tarmac our front drive. They said they were working in the area and could do it for half the usual price.'

I said, 'I'm just back from an expedition to the North Pole.'

'Fancy. But you'd think they'd know we had more sense than to fall for that, a cock-and-bull story about having some tarmac left over. My husband reported them to the police but they weren't interested.'

'Don't you want to know whether we saw Father Christmas?'

'Ha-ha. Funny you should say that, I think our daughter still believes in Santa Claus. When she was about twelve I tried to tell her it was her dad who answered the letters she addressed to Santa and drank the glass of sweet sherry she left by the fireplace. She was so upset, I've not dared to broach the subject since.'

I persisted. 'We had a few narrow escapes. I nearly fell down a crevasse.'

'Goodness. Reminds me of the only time I went skiing and slid off the ski run. I found myself up to my waist in deep snow. It took me ages to struggle back and we never went skiing again. And the worst thing was that when we got back we found the dog had been taken ill at the kennels. It cost us a fortune in vet's fees.'

Undaunted, I tried again when we next met. After our customary tame exchanges about the weather I said, 'I'm off to see my father again today. I sat with him all day yesterday. He's on his deathbed.'

'Gracious. My father didn't hang around, he dropped dead with an aneurysm, but my aunt – that's my mother's sister – lingered for ages. She was unconscious for two days before she died. My sister and I sat by her bedside doing our knitting. She never even knew we were there.'

It was hopeless. No questions about my father: where was he? Why was he dying? How old was he? Was I close to him?

The score was zilch.

Shortly after this encounter, Glenda vanished. I felt slightly annoyed that I'd been deprived of further attempts to cajole a question out of her, especially as I'd dreamt up some promising scenarios: how I was once kidnapped and spent a year chained to a radiator; how I was an accidental bigamist; how I'd made a fortune but lost it all gambling; how I'd got lost in the Amazon rainforest; how I'd walked across Niagara Falls on a tightrope. Things like that.

Naturally I wondered what had become of Glenda but quickly pushed speculations aside, fearful that even thinking about her might conjure her up. My walks continued and I met another dog walker, a woman with whom it was possible to have normal two-way conversations.

Then one morning I tethered my dog to the metal ring outside the newsagent and, as usual, collected my daily paper. Glenda's obituary was on page fifteen. I read how she and her dog had been mown down by a lorry whilst crossing a main road. Both had died at the scene. The obituary went on to describe her 'glittering career' as an economist, first at Coutts Bank and eventually as head of the UK Government's Economic Unit. A photograph showed her being awarded a CBE by the Queen at Buckingham Palace. I read the caption.

The investiture had happened only two years before Glenda and I had met.

Why, I wondered, after I'd given her so many opportunities, had she never once mentioned her illustrious career?

I could hear her saying, 'Because you never asked.'

The Encounter

They met in the bar after attending the first day of a government-sponsored conference on trauma and domestic abuse.

Unfortunately the day had not lived up to expectations. The hotel conference room, designed to double up as a banqueting hall or ballroom, had magnificent chandeliers but no windows. The glorious autumn day, trees ablaze with leaves on the turn, had passed by unseen by the delegates. Lunch had been too rushed and the buffet had run out of salad. Coffee and tea breaks had been chaos, with insufficient staff serving and long queues forming.

The speakers, mostly men despite an overwhelming majority of the 230 delegates being women, had inflicted too many PowerPoints on a passive audience. Timekeeping had been poor, with presentations often overrunning their allotted time slots, and the Q&A sessions were either severely truncated or axed. Questions from the floor were often inaudible, delegates either failing to wait for the roving mike to reach them or, when it did, not speaking into it clearly. In their confusion some people even switched off the microphone, convinced they were switching it on.

When the day's proceedings eventually drew to a close, Reginald retreated to his room on the fifth floor and took a lengthy shower with the water going full pelt. Feeling refreshed, he dutifully phoned home and, having learnt that all was well, went for a walk along the canal towpath before dinner.

As he walked in the twilight, relishing the fresh air and reflecting on what he'd gleaned from the day's sessions, he passed a woman who looked vaguely familiar. Half a mile later, he recalled where he'd seen her before: at the conference during the morning break whilst he stood in the coffee queue struggling to open a stubborn packet of ginger biscuits. He remembered she had been standing alone, engrossed in sending text messages on her smartphone.

He thought no more about her until he entered the bar after dinner. There she was again, sitting by herself at a small table with what looked like a brandy. She was still sending text messages and he admired the way her thumbs flicked, apparently effortlessly over the keys.

She was the only person sitting alone. All the other tables were taken by delegates from the conference reminiscing about the day's proceedings, the hubbub of voices occasionally punctuated by explosions of laugher. Reginald ordered a drink from the bar but hesitated to join the woman and interrupt her texting. While he dithered about where to sit, she looked up and smiled. 'Do join me,' she said, indicating a nearby chair.

'You look busy, I didn't like to interrupt,' said Reginald.

'Oh, I'll be glad of the distraction. I'm a life coach and I've got clients who've been pestering me all day.'

'Pestering you? I'm sorry to hear that.'

'Yes, one has been traumatised since she saw a mouse in her kitchen. It's pathetic. The silly cow seems to have spent most of the day standing on a chair. Another has had a row with her partner and he's gone off to the pub. She knows he'll be violent when he gets back. I've told her to pack a case and bugger off. And now I keep getting texts from a woman who is threatening to kill herself. I've told her not to be silly. My name's Harriet, by the way, Harriet Robinson.' She thrust out her hand and Reginald took it compliantly.

'How do you do. I'm Reginald Bucknall. I take it that you didn't tell your clients you were going to be away for a couple of days?'

'They know they can contact me any time, day or night, wherever I am. All part of the service, I'm afraid. No peace for the wicked.'

'Hmm, that wouldn't suit me,' said Reginald. 'We don't offer an emergency service and we aren't allowed to give clients our contact details. If they want to get in touch, they have to make an appointment via the office.'

'Sounds very bureaucratic. What charity is that?'

'Relate,' said Reginald uneasily, feeling he was being drawn into betraying a confidence.

'Well,' Harriet snapped, 'you should thank your lucky stars that you don't have clients like mine! Dependent wimps!' She glanced down momentarily at her phone then looked up and asked, 'Tell me, what did you make of today's proceedings?'

'A bit like the curate's egg I suppose,' said Reginald warily. 'Good in parts.'

Harriet pulled a face. 'An utter shambles! And far too much

emphasis on all that namby-pamby person-centred stuff for my liking. I skipped most of the afternoon.'

Harriet was a heavy, rather blowsy woman in her late fifties. Her hair was dyed blonde and she had a tight mouth with a protruding jaw. Without being asked, she told Reginald that she had set up as an independent coach five years ago when her career in social services had been cut short after an enquiry had found her negligent in a case of child abuse.

'Not my fault,' Harriet insisted. 'The child's mother was a manipulative bitch. She concealed the fact that she'd taken in a new partner who was an alcoholic with anger-management problems. No one knew.'

'How distressing,' said Reginald. 'What happened to the child?'

'Died of a brain haemorrhage a few days after being admitted to hospital with head injuries and numerous broken bones. The enquiry criticised the lack of "joined-up thinking" between the support services but, as the lead social worker, I got blamed. I was the bloody scapegoat.'

'I'm so sorry,' said Reginald empathetically. 'A real setback.'

'Not really. As it turned out, it was the best thing that could have happened.' Harriet chuckled to herself. 'If I hadn't got the push, I'd still be an underpaid social worker with an impossible case load.'

Reginald, taken aback at Harriet's lack of contrition, didn't like to probe any further. He just nodded and said, 'Funny you should say that. Over the years I've known a number of people who were made redundant. Even though it seemed a disaster at the time, they bounced back by getting a better job or starting up on their own.'

'Yes, I've no regrets. Have a look at my website and read the testimonials.' With a flourish, Harriet produced her business card and pushed it across the table towards Reginald. 'What about you? Has your path run smoothly?'

'Yes, I've been lucky. I was a teacher, deputy head of a comprehensive, but I took early retirement at sixty, did voluntary work as a Samaritan for a couple of years and then I trained as a marriage guidance counsellor. Keeps me out of mischief.'

'Can't say I envy you,' said Harriet. 'I could never be a Samaritan, don't hold with all that listening stuff. My clients pay me good money to tell them things they don't want to hear. I give them no-nonsense advice.'

Reginald was nonplussed. 'That's interesting. I take it you're not a fan of the non-directive approach?'

'Fuck no, forgive my French. I don't hold with all that wishy-washy, client-centred stuff.' Harriet sat back as if to say 'so there!' and sipped her brandy.

Reginald, astonished by Harriet's forthrightness, kept his calm. 'Well, in that case I'm not surprised you skipped the afternoon. One of the more interesting sessions gave recent research findings showing that clients were far more forthcoming when the counsellor employed active listening. Apparently, on average, it encourages clients to say twice as much.'

'Oh, for God's sake! Who the hell wants clients to do more talking?'

Wishing he'd chosen to sit somewhere else, Reginald persisted gently. 'As I understand it, the whole point of encouraging clients to talk is to help them put things into perspective and work towards finding their own solutions.'

Harriet shook her head in disbelief. 'Utter claptrap! Giving people a shoulder to cry on may make them feel better in the short term, but it solves nothing. My clients want some tough love, to be challenged. They need to see how their self-defeating beliefs are the root of all their problems.'

Reginald's heart sank. He had come into the bar for a quiet nightcap before retiring; he felt irritated that he had found himself caught up in conversation with this aggressive woman. He had always dreaded confrontation and had spent his life leaning over backwards to avoid it. As a deputy head, he'd often had to deal with angry parents complaining about this and that. He'd always found it best to listen patiently to their gripes until they ran out of steam.

'Well,' said Reginald noncommittally, 'each to his own I suppose.' He looked at his watch. 'Goodness, is that the time? I must turn in. An early start tomorrow.'

He started to get to his feet but it wasn't easy; his chair was low and the cushion squishy.

Harriet put out a restraining arm. 'Hang on a mo! You can't duck out leaving things up in the air like that.' She leaned forward and looked straight into Reginald's eyes. 'Where does marriage guidance stand? Do you use behavioural therapy?'

Reginald, desperate to leave but feeling he should attempt to defend Relate, sank back into his seat. 'We used to concentrate on marriage, but our work is broader now and covers all sorts of relationships. We try to provide a safe space for people to talk through their difficulties…' His voice trailed off. He felt utterly inadequate under Harriet's unflinching gaze.

'Ah-ha,' said Harriet gleefully. 'I suspected as much! You stay on the fence, offering no guidance, no actual advice.'

'I'm not sure that's quite fair,' Reginald spluttered. 'We

believe in empowering people to work towards their own solutions.'

Harriet sat back triumphantly. 'Just as I thought, more of that crappy non-judgemental stuff!'

Reginald, who was not a large man, managed to stagger to his feet.

Harriet remained seated. 'I bet you go in for all that mindfulness mumbo-jumbo too,' she snorted.

A wave of anger spread through Reginald's body, like pressure building in a volcano that had been inactive for years. It was an alien feeling he hadn't experienced since, as a schoolboy, he'd lashed out at someone who had teased him for coming last in a cross-country race.

Before he knew what he was doing, Reginald bent down until his face drew level with Harriet's. He shrieked, 'You piss me off!' and marched out of the room. Conversations in the bar stopped abruptly and heads turned to see who was doing the shouting.

The next morning Reginald rose early, packed and left for home without having breakfast. Safely on the train, he gazed out of the window and succumbed to an uncontrollable fit of giggles. Tears rolled down his cheeks as he reflected on the irony of him, of all people, giving someone a blast of judgemental feedback.

He had to admit, it felt good. Very good.

The Eulogy

The church was packed. Music lovers had travelled from far and wide to celebrate the life of the controversial musicologist, Dr Richard Jiggle. The memorial service, held three months after his untimely death, had been widely publicised. Extra chairs were hurriedly arranged in the side aisles once it became clear they were needed to prevent people having to stand or, worse still, be denied entry. The sun illuminated the stained-glass windows on the south side of the church, casting a kaleidoscope of abstract patterns onto the stone pillars of the nave.

The congregation was not only large, it was unusually diverse. The late Dr Jiggle's family members, a sister and a brother together with their offspring (Dr Jiggle had never married), were joined by his academic colleagues who, perched on the unforgiving wooden pews, sat shoulder to shoulder with Dr Jiggle's numerous fans: regular concert-goers from the Barbican who loved, and in many cases collected, his irreverent programme notes, and holidaymakers on cruises who had been enthralled by his lectures.

Dr Jiggle would have been delighted with the turnout. He had always relished entertaining captive audiences, particularly those gathered together, drinks in hand, in the sumptuous lounges of luxury cruise liners. At the time of his death, his popularity as a speaker on classical music and the lives of composers was at its height.

There were two eulogies. The first was delivered by Dr Jiggle's sister. Unlike her late brother, who had been overweight and unkempt, she was a neat, small woman, dwarfed by the brass eagle lectern with its generous wings.

The top of her head bobbed up and down as she read an account of her brother's happy childhood in Dorset and how, despite almost certainly being dyslexic, he had taught himself to read music at an early age. He had learnt to play the piano and the 'cello, gaining distinctions in both at grade eight. She recounted how it slowly dawned on him that he wasn't cut out for a career as a performer; he was too gregarious to shut himself away practising for eight hours a day. He had won a scholarship to Cambridge and gained an MA in musicology.

People in the congregation, relishing their memories of Dr Jiggle as a cheerful, larger-than-life character, were incredulous that his sister could be so dull. There had been ample opportunities for histrionics, but her delivery was dry and humourless. They gazed at the cover of the order of service where a large photograph of Dr Jiggle, wearing a skew-whiff bow tie, beamed happily at them. They longed for him to rise from the dead and deliver his own eulogy.

After Dr Jiggle's sister had spoken, and 'Blessed Are the Poor in Heart' had been sung (Dr Jiggle had left a list of his favourite hymns and organ music), a tall, distinguished-looking man rose from his pew and strode to the lectern. This was Sir Vernon Hamilton, a long-time colleague of Dr Jiggle's at the school of music.

Sir Vernon stood, calmly surveying the congregation as he gathered his thoughts. 'Ladies and gentlemen, as many of you will know, Richard, my late colleague, was a brilliant lecturer.' His voice was deep and strong. 'Richard had an uncanny ability to adjust his delivery to suit the wavelength of his listeners. One of his many maxims was "know your audience" and, with that in mind, I'm going to ask you to indicate by raising your hand into which of two categories you primarily fall. Firstly, those of you who enjoyed Richard's programme notes and/or knew Richard as a popular speaker on cruise ships.'

Hands shot up from at least three-quarters of the congregation. In their enthusiasm, some even waved both hands.

Sir Vernon smiled. 'Thank you. And secondly, Richard's students, past and present, and his colleagues from academia.'

About a quarter of the hands were raised.

'Just as I thought, we have a church full of fans!' He shouted the word 'fans' as if he were introducing an act at the London Palladium. A restrained cheer went up – restrained only because people were unsure how demonstrative to be within the hallowed walls of the church.

Sir Vernon beamed approvingly. 'I'll do my best to address what I have to say to the vast majority here, namely those of you who admired Richard as an entertaining storyteller.'

The congregation settled down as comfortably as the oak pews would allow. Some were using the embroidered kneelers as cushions. The church bells chimed half-past the hour.

Sir Vernon continued. 'It's fair to say that Richard had a low boredom threshold.' People laughed, appreciating the under-statement. 'He wrote the Barbican's programme notes for a number of years without mishap, but eventually he started to include deliberate mistakes to see if anyone would notice. Initially the mistakes were minor – an incorrect birth date or place, for example, or a contrived middle name. However, factual mistakes like these were usually corrected by the proof reader and Richard realised he'd have to be – how can I put it? – more creative.'

Members of the congregation smiled to themselves, as if to say 'here we go'.

Sir Vernon cleared his throat and went on. 'As those of you who were avid collectors of his programme notes will know, his campaign to attract attention exceeded his expec-tations. Soon hundreds of concertgoers were caught up in a "spot-Richard's-mistakes" game. It was an undoubted win-win: Richard basked in his newfound notoriety and the Barbican's programmes became collectors' items.'

Sir Vernon paused. He wasn't speaking from notes and he moved away from the shelter of the lectern, instead standing tall and exposed on the steps to the chancel.

'Of the many fictions Richard dreamed up, perhaps the most outrageous was the story he spun about Beethoven and Schubert. Despite both composers living in Vienna and moving in the same circles, there is no evidence that they ever met. Beethoven was a celebrity in his lifetime and it is unlikely that Schubert, twenty-three years his junior, had either the courage or the opportunity to make himself known to the master.'

Some members of the congregation exchanged knowing glances. Sir Vernon, confident he had everyone's attention, continued. 'However, as many of you will know, shortly before his death Richard claimed to have unearthed evidence that the two composers not only met in 1822, five years before Beethoven's death, but that Beethoven secretly commissioned Schubert to ghost write some of his late string quartets. Richard claimed that the deal meant that Beethoven, by then not only deaf but also stressed and in ill health, was freed up to concentrate on composing his ambitious Ninth Symphony. Furthermore, according to Richard, the secret agreement explained why Schubert discontinued work on his own eighth symphony: the Unfinished.'

Suddenly a strident woman's voice called out from the gallery, 'Has Richard's claim that there was a secret agreement between the two men been totally discredited?'

Astonished at the interruption, people turned and gazed up at the gallery, straining to see who had spoken. Before Sir Vernon could respond, a man in the front pew stood up and turned to face the congregation.

'I am a professor at the Royal School of Music. Much as it may disappoint you, I can assure you that there is absolutely no truth in my late colleague's story. It was a complete fabrication. Richard was warned to desist from inventing such stories and bringing our profession into disrepute or face the consequences.'

An elderly man shouted, 'Absolutely disgraceful! You lot are just jealous of his success. You should be ashamed of yourselves, hounding the poor man to his death.'

'Yes!' screamed the woman from the gallery. 'You only have yourselves to blame. You have his blood on your hands!'

Someone else called out, 'I wouldn't be surprised to hear

that one of you pushed him overboard.' A number of people clapped in agreement and some shouted 'hear, hear'.

Attempting to regain control of the proceedings, Sir Vernon, said, 'Ladies and gentlemen, nothing would delight me more than to be able to use this occasion to announce that Richard's theory had been authenticated but, as Professor Jenkins has said, I fear it was nothing more than one of Richard's entertaining stories.'

'Prove it!' shouted a new voice.

Professor Jenkins, looking flushed, leapt up again and yelled, 'There is nothing to prove, absolutely *nothing*! The whole story is utter nonsense.'

'Sit down!' someone called out. 'You're not helping. We enjoyed Richard's stories, a bit of harmless fun.'

The canon, who had been conducting the service before mayhem broke out, stood and raised his arms in a bid to calm the proceedings. 'Ladies and gentlemen, please remember we are in God's house and gathered together to celebrate Dr Jiggle's remarkable life. Might I suggest we regain our composure by singing the next hymn, "Dear Lord and Father of Mankind, Forgive Our Foolish Ways".'

The organ struck up. Sir Vernon shrugged his shoulders in capitulation and returned to his seat with as much dignity as he could muster. The congregation reluctantly struggled to their feet and the hymn was duly sung, albeit half-heartedly.

Thereafter the canon kept a tight grip on the proceedings and the remainder of the service passed without incident.

In the weeks following the disorderly memorial service, two significant things happened. Firstly, a coroner's inquest into Dr Jiggle's untimely death brought in an open verdict. No one could explain how he could have fallen off a luxury liner on a calm night and drowned in the Mediterranean. The circumstances of his death at the age of sixty-three remained a mystery.

Secondly, a small piece appeared in *The Times* under the headline 'Dissonant musicologists'. It recounted how a secret compartment had been discovered in an antique writing desk that had belonged to the late musicologist, Dr Richard Jiggle. Documents found in the compartment confirmed that the desk had once been the property of Anton Diabelli, an Austrian music publisher who had died in Vienna in 1858. Apparently, amongst the documents was a note in Diabelli's handwriting, dated 18 November 1822, describing how he had introduced the young Schubert to Beethoven 'with a view to Beethoven using Schubert to share his load'.

The article finished with a quote from a Professor Jenkins. 'This is an astonishing and totally unexpected find. Until now it has always been assumed that the two composers never met. If they did, it helps to explain why Schubert was a torch bearer at Beethoven's funeral. It is no exaggeration to say that the discovery of these documents is unprecedented and some – or all – of Beethoven's late string quartets, despite the original scores being in his hand, may have to be reattributed.'

The Expert

The invitation was totally unexpected: an envelope from the BBC, addressed to him care of his publisher. Why, he wondered, would his licence renewal be sent to his publisher? Fred turned the envelope over in his rough hands and carefully slit the envelope open with a knife. The letter inside was brief.

Dear Mr Fred Bambridge

We are exploring the feasibility of making a television programme about root vegetables. The programme is still at the conceptual stage but we envisage an interview format, with experts being quizzed on the merits of eating more root vegetables.

We have read, and much enjoyed, your book on turnips and swedes and hope you will agree to be one of our advisers on the development of the programme.

If this is of interest, please telephone me on the above number.

Yours sincerely
Suzanne Brown
Commissioning Editor, BBC Food Programmes

He read the letter again and studied the signature, a large S followed by a generous squiggle. He was surprised that anyone at the Beeb knew about his book; published six years earlier with a modest print run, it was now out of print.

He read the letter twice more. What, he wondered, was involved in being an adviser? And who might the other advisers be?

He decided, as he always did with life's big decisions, to ponder the invitation. If, having slept on it, he remained curious, he'd contact the BBC and find out more. He put the letter back in its envelope and pinned it to the notice board in the kitchen. He adjusted the envelope so that it was absolutely straight, pulled on his wellies and, humming tunelessly, went out to tend his root vegetables.

Fred, a widower for the past eight years, was in his early sixties and lived alone. At the age of fifty he had been made redundant by British Steel, where he'd worked since leaving school. His long years of service resulted in a generous redundancy package, which he'd used to purchase a smallholding of nearly two acres on the outskirts of Sheffield. This was where he indulged his passion for growing organic root vegetables. Over the years he had built up a successful one-man business supplying local supermarkets.

He had written his book to while away the lonely hours after his wife died and, to his surprise, it had been published. From time to time he received letters from readers asking questions:

Are neeps swedes or turnips?

Are swedes turnips that have been grown in Sweden?

Can you eat turnip leaves and, if so, how do you get rid of the bitter taste?

How much sugar is there in a turnip?

When did people start eating turnips?

He always replied by writing on the letter, 'Thank you for your enquiry. You'll find the answer to your question on page (so and so) of my book.' He then posted the letter back to the sender, wondering whether one day he might be asked a question that was not covered somewhere in his book.

After a couple of days, Fred telephoned Suzanne Brown and, sounding suitably non-committal, agreed to attend an exploratory meeting at the BBC offices in Manchester. He was assured that his travelling expenses would be reimbursed.

As Fred travelled to the meeting by train, he gazed out of the window at sodden fields. Two young people, who introduced themselves as Nigel and Julia, collected him from the reception area. Suzanne Brown was nowhere to be seen. As they guided Fred to the meeting room on the first floor, Nigel explained that, if the programme went ahead, he would be the director and Julia the producer. The difference between the two roles was not explained and Fred didn't like to ask.

When they reached the meeting room two people were already there, chatting happily: a man called Bill, an authority on potatoes, and a large, opinionated lady called Laura who, it seemed, knew everything there was to know about onions.

Nigel thanked them for coming. 'I'm keen to have your input so that Julia and I can make a convincing case for a thir-ty-minute programme about root vegetables – what they are, how to grow them, how to cook them and how to enjoy them.'

Ideas came thick and fast, admittedly mostly from Laura and Bill with Fred chipping in whenever they paused to draw breath. Julia, armed with felt-tipped pens, made notes on large sheets of flip-chart paper. After an hour or so Nigel professed himself delighted with their help. 'Thank you. We now have more than enough material to put together a theme paper. I'll send you all a draft so that you can comment before it is finalised.'

Fred went back to his smallholding and continued to tend his root vegetables. The post came and went with nothing further from the BBC. As the weeks passed, Fred's disappointment faded but he remained irritated. He couldn't forgive himself for succumbing to flattery and allowing his expectations to be raised.

Eventually, long after Fred had given up expecting to hear anything further, a letter from the BBC arrived.

Dear Fred,

Apologies for the delay in getting back to you following our meeting a few months ago. I had hoped to get the enclosed script to you well before now. I'm pleased to be able to tell you that we now have the go-ahead and are in a position to finalise arrangements for the programme.

We would like to invite you to participate in the proposed interview, and I am authorised to offer you a fee of £1,000 plus expenses.

Please sign the enclosed contract and return it to me at your earliest convenience. I look forward to working with you on this project.

Your sincerely
Julia Bucknell
Producer, Root Vegetable Project.

Fred was amazed: they wanted him to *appear* in the programme, not just to advise on the contents! He was wary yet intrigued. He read through the script and grudgingly admitted that it was rather good. He studied the contract, reading and rereading the small print to look for snags but found none. After mulling it over for a few days, he signed and dated the contract, then returned it to the BBC in the stamped addressed envelope they had provided.

Two more lengthy meetings followed with Laura, Bill and Fred going through the script carefully, suggesting modifications. None of them had been on television before but Nigel assured them that the interviewer, a well-known newsreader, would look after them and steer them through the scripted questions. It wasn't necessary to learn their answers by heart; they merely needed to be familiar with the questions they'd be asked so that there were no surprises. Fred was relieved to hear this. He was happy to ad lib as long as he knew in advance what he was going to be asked.

The day for recording the programme arrived. Fred, in his best Sunday suit, got to the studio in good time. Outwardly he appeared calm but, in truth, inside he was churning with a mixture of apprehension and excitement. Bill and Laura were chatting away nervously.

They were all escorted into the studio. Four chairs were arranged in a semi-circle, one for each of them, with the fourth chair reserved for the absent newsreader. Cables snaked across the floor, unfamiliar lights came on and off, and cameramen sat behind huge cameras on wheels waiting patiently to swing into action. Nigel and Julia prowled around clutching clipboards, glancing anxiously at the clock on the studio wall. Nigel assured them that the newscaster would soon be with them.

A pretty girl powdered Fred's bald patch and nose and adjusted his collar. A sound engineer clipped a microphone to the lapel of his jacket with a warning not to touch it accidentally with hand gestures. Bill and Laura fell uncharacteristically silent. Cameras zoomed in and out doing practice runs. Julia was talking quietly on her mobile behind a cupped hand. Time ticked away.

Eventually the famous newscaster swept in. He offered no explanation or apology for cutting things fine. Nigel and Julia looked relieved that he had arrived and fussed round him deferentially. The makeup girls swung into action.

He asked for a copy of the script and a pencil. He flicked through the pages, crossing things out and saying, 'Surely you don't expect me to ask this?' and 'Who on earth wrote this stuff?' Fred assumed this was some sort of friendly banter between professionals but was surprised when Nigel and Julia demurred, assuring the newscaster that the scripted questions, so carefully crafted over a series of meetings, were merely a guide.

The countdown began and a red light came on. They were live.

The newscaster spoke directly to the camera and introduced the panel. He was within his element, charming and totally at ease; it was as if he'd flicked a switch. He turned to Laura with a big smile and asked her a question about parsnips. She gave an answer as best she could, but added that she knew more about onions than parsnips.

Undaunted, the newscaster asked Bill an unscripted question about carrots. Bill gulped but managed to produce a satisfactory answer. The newscaster then turned to Fred but, before he could ask whatever he was about to ask, Fred unclipped his microphone and walked out of the studio and into the Manchester rain.

The Goody-goody

My name is Emma and, unlikely as it seems, I have just whacked my boss with a heavy reference book. He was taken unawares and he stumbled and hit his head on the edge of a metal bookshelf. I think he's dead. I haven't seen a dead person before, but he doesn't seem to be breathing and has gone a funny colour. There's a pool of blood on the carpet too. It definitely doesn't look good.

If you knew me, I'm sure you would realise I'm not the sort of person to kill someone – let alone my boss just after we'd locked up after a routine day. For a start, I'm a small person, only five foot four inches in my stockinged feet and skinny too. My boss is over six feet tall and certainly weighs fifteen stone, maybe more. (Should I be saying was? I'm not sure. He looks the same height and weight as he did when he was alive.)

Not only am I physically small, I'm also a quiet, unassuming person. The sort of person who wouldn't say boo to a goose. I went to a co-ed school and the teachers were always telling me I shouldn't be so meek and mild, should assert myself. The only time I took their advice I finished up being humiliated.

In assembly one day the head teacher asked us what MP stood for. My dad was in the army so I knew the answer was military police. My hand shot up and I shouted out the answer. Everyone laughed and the head teacher told me I was wrong; the correct answer was Member of Parliament. But how can that be right? Member of Parliament would be MOP, wouldn't it?

I suppose I ought to do something about my boss. Cover him up or something? Or ring for an ambulance?

I've always found men difficult. I've got two brothers, both older than me – Bill four years older and Chris two. I was the baby of the family. My dad, an army sergeant, used to hit my mum but he left home when I was ten. Just said he was going to get petrol and never came back. During their teenage years my brothers grew huge, both finishing up well over six feet tall. They were keen on sports and played football for the local club. I wasn't at all sporty.

For as long as I can remember my brothers teased me. When I was thirteen they used to show off their muscles doing push-ups and hanging from door frames dressed only in their underpants. Sometimes, when my mum was out, they'd show me their erections to shock me. I knew I shouldn't react, just ignore it, but I'd get upset and lock myself in my bedroom. They'd laugh and hammer on the door. I never told my mum. I was too embarrassed.

My secondary school was co-ed but, because I was small for my age and a bit of a swot, I'm glad to say the boys mostly ignored me. Most of the girls in my class had grown breasts and wore short skirts. They were always giggling about their exploits with boyfriends. But I was a late developer and boys never chatted me up. I wore glasses too.

I left school with good GCSEs and A levels and went to work in the local library to train as a library assistant. You'd think a library was a calm place, but not with a boss like mine. He was always uptight, finding fault with everything. Even though I was usually blameless, he'd pick on me as the most junior member of staff. Nothing I did was ever good enough: books put back on the wrong shelves, fines not collected, the kitchenette untidy, customers making a noise when I was supposed to keep them quiet, people stealing books – all my fault. It didn't help that the council kept cutting the budget and threatening to close the library and sell off the building.

I don't know why I'm sitting here so calmly typing this on my laptop. A displacement activity, I suppose. Perhaps I should phone 999? But that would raise the alarm and people would come and make a fuss. It's nice and quiet in here, exactly the way a library should be. Just lots of books, me and my boss lying still over there.

My dad was a big bloke too. He was always shouting at my mum, complaining about everything. He used to hit her if she answered back. After he left, my mum had to go out to work so things weren't easy at home, and my two brothers were untidy and never did enough to help. They used to step out of their clothes and leave them in a heap on the floor. Same with their football kit. The bathroom was always a mess too, with towels not hung up and the floor left soaking wet after they'd had a shower. I did my best to help my mum with household chores and my brothers called me a goody-goody.

The mobile phone belonging to my boss has just pinged. He'd left it on his desk. I had a look and it's a text message from his wife asking when he'll be home. I've sent a reply, 'Sorry, but something's come up and I'm working late. I'll let you know when I'm on my way'. I was tempted to say, 'Hello, it's me. I'm afraid your husband is dead. He was a bad-tempered bastard and I hit him with a book'. But I thought better of it.

I was sure that working in a library would suit me. I've always loved books and reading, and I did a lot of swotting for my A Levels in my local library. It got me out of the house and away from my noisy brothers. So coming here and getting harassed was a nasty shock, not at all what I'd imagined. I didn't even have a honeymoon period. He picked on me straight away, yelling at me in front of volunteers and customers. I never answered back, just tried to do things better and reduce the criticism. But my boss was never satisfied. Kept on and on.

Come to think of it, this is the first time he's stopped getting at me. Killing him has certainly led to a dramatic improvement in his behaviour. An hour of blissful silence so far. Funny thing was that the book I hit him with wasn't that big – *Encyclopaedia Britannica, Volume 8*. I've put it back where it belongs between volumes seven and nine.

Hang on, his mobile phone is ringing now. I suppose I'd better answer it…

***

A month has passed, rather a busy month as things turned out! It was his wife on the phone and I told her that her husband had met with an accident and that I was about to phone for an ambulance. She asked me if I was trained in first aid. I said not, so she told me to stay put until help arrived.

She got to the library before the police arrived and, in the circumstances, I thought she was admirably calm. She took one look at her husband and then asked me if I was alright. Of course the police had lots of questions. I didn't tell them that I'd hit him, just that he'd fallen and hit his head on the metal shelving. The post-mortem found he'd had a massive stroke.

So, to cut a long story short, I'm back at the library reporting to a temporary boss while a new one is recruited. They told me I needed to get more experience before I could be considered. I'm booked to do a first-aid course and my new boss is a vast improvement: kind, considerate and appreciative. The funny thing is that the other day, when he was passing the reference section, he remarked that the *Encyclopaedia Britannica* was a waste of space now that everything was on the internet. I didn't like to tell him how volume eight had transformed my life.

The Hon. Treasurer

The treasurer sat, as he always did, on the chairman's immediate left. He looked exactly like a treasurer should: bald, clean shaven, half glasses, a dark blazer with brass buttons, a tie that would not look out of place at a funeral, polished shoes – an hon. treasurer from tip to toe.

Whilst quietly excited at the prospect of the bombshell he was about to drop, his expression gave nothing away. His papers were arranged neatly in front of him and close at hand was a four-ring binder containing copies of the club's accounts stretching back twelve years or more.

The treasurer, his name was Trevor Dunn, remained silent as the minutes of the previous meeting were scrutinised. Small amendments were made; a date corrected, an action allocated, some commas inserted here and there. Finally the minutes were agreed and signed as an accurate record of the proceedings. Throughout 'matters arising', the treasurer continued to sit passively, arms crossed, astonished that such trifles could take so long and stir such passions.

Eventually the chairman turned to him and called for the treasurer's report. 'Over to you, Trevor. Finances in good shape?'

The treasurer glanced around the table, checking that he had the undivided attention of his colleagues. He slowly uncrossed his arms, leaned forward and cleared his throat. His moment had come.

'Gentlemen, I trust you have studied the accounts I circulated before the meeting. You will see that I have shown expenditure to date against the current budget and, in the column on the right, a comparison with last year's expenditure at this time.'

Papers were rustled and everyone nodded.

'The only major disparity, and certainly a cause for concern, is the cost of engraving the trophies. You will see that the figure has more than doubled. I have investigated why this has occurred, and it seems that the engraver we have used for many years has unfortunately had to retire through ill health – incurable cancer, I believe.' The treasurer paused to allow the gravity of the situation to sink in. 'Anyway, his son has now taken over the business. We had no advanced warning of any increase in the engraving costs. The first I knew of it was when the invoice arrived.'

He paused again to allow the outrage to register.

'When I telephoned to query the increase, the new owner explained he had discovered that his father had given us a heavily discounted rate for many years and that this could not continue.'

'And you say we received no warning, no notification at all?' asked the chairman.

'No, sadly none. As you can imagine, when the invoice arrived it was a considerable shock.'

'Must have been, must have been. Have you paid the invoice?'

'You will be pleased to hear that I have succeeded in negotiating a twenty-percent reduction. However, the new owner has made it clear that this is a one-off concession and that the preferential treatment extended to us in the past cannot continue.'

A member of the committee, Brigadier Basil Thornton-Jones, in charge of lawns and equipment, cleared his throat. 'Mr Chairman, this is clearly disgraceful. Hiking prices without due warning is not, in my experience, good business practice.' The brigadier shook his head sadly. 'Not good at all. May I propose that we put the engraving out to tender so that we can compare rates and, if need be, engage new engravers?'

'Capital idea, Brigadier, capital,' said the chairman, beaming his approval.

The room grew dark as a white cloud temporarily obscured the sun outside.

'Mr Chairman,' said the treasurer, 'I trust you won't think me presumptuous, but I have already made enquiries and can confirm that the invoice from the engraver is, in fact, competitive. The going rate for engraving silver trophies such as ours is £12.75 for a set-up fee and 12p per letter thereafter.'

'Good Lord,' said the brigadier. 'Surely that's outrageous. When I win a trophy, which as you know is fairly often, that's going to cost... Hang on while I work it out.'

The treasurer's fingers were already dancing over the keys of his calculator like those of a concert pianist at a Steinway. 'That's twenty-eight letters at 12p each, plus the set-up fee of £12.75, giving a total of £16.11.'

'I've a horrible idea mine will pip yours, Basil,' said Sir Christopher Gilderdale-Scott, the committee member in charge of arranging fixtures with other clubs.

'Yes,' confirmed the treasurer, revelling in the opportunity to demonstrate his prowess on the calculator. 'Yours would come to £12.75 plus £3.60, a total of £16.35.'

The committee members fell silent as they absorbed these staggering figures.

'How many trophies do we have?' asked the newest member of the committee, a gentleman called Dr Algernon Westmacott-Hill.

'Sixteen in total,' said the chairman.

'Amounting to £204 in set-up fees alone,' added the treasurer.

'The problem,' said the chairman, whose name was George Beaumont-Brearley, 'is that lots of our members have double-barrelled names. Why, even mine is twenty-two letters long.'

'Forgive me, Mr Chairman, twenty-three letters long. You have forgotten the hyphen,' corrected the treasurer.

The brigadier, his moustache twitching and no longer able to contain himself, exclaimed, 'Surely the wretched fellow doesn't count a dash as a letter? Unacceptable, totally unacceptable!'

Committee members muttered their assent.

'Gentlemen,' said the chairman, 'I know this has been a shock but I must call you to order. I suggest that, now we have been apprised of the facts, we postpone further discussion until we meet again in December. Please reflect on the problem and come to the next meeting with your suggestions.'

And without further ado, the chairman closed the meeting and the committee members left the room looking suitably sombre. Outside the day was warm, a classic Indian summer's day. Leaves from the chestnut trees fluttered lazily and settled on the lawns. The hands of the clock on the gable of the wooden sports pavilion, built in 1909, approached half-past twelve. Some committee members adjourned to the club house bar for G&Ts to revive their spirits before lunch.

Two months later, on a wild December day with the chestnut trees swaying as if they were drunk and sudden gusts of wind sending leaves scurrying across the lawns in agitated flurries, the chairman welcomed everyone to the second meeting. The anticipation in the room was palpable. The minutes of the previous meeting were hurriedly agreed and the chairman opened the main agenda item: the thorny issue of the escalating engraving costs.

'Gentlemen, we need to agree how best to take things forward.'

Ideas came thick and fast.

'Raise the annual subscription to cover the increase in engraving costs.'

'Reduce the number of competitions.'

'Award trophies but do not have them engraved.'

'Members to pay to have their name engraved on the trophies they win.'

The hon. treasurer chipped in. 'How about making it a rule that members with long names can't enter competitions? Or, if they do, they must agree not to win.'

'Absolutely not!' exclaimed Brigadier Basil Thornton-Jones. 'Absurdly discriminatory. You're only suggesting that because you have a short name. Not on, not on.'

'Then,' said Trevor, feeling mischievous, 'how about insisting that winners with long, double-barrelled names shorten them?'

The last idea caught people's imagination.

'Oh, what fun!' said Sir Christopher Gilderdale-Scott. 'I could be Sir Chris, eight letters instead of thirty. A considerable saving.'

'And I could be Brig Basil, nine letters instead of twenty-eight,' the brigadier offered.

'Why,' said the chairman, not to be out done, 'Instead of George Beaumont-Brearley I could use the nickname I had at my prep school, Porgy. Just five letters. Can anyone beat that?'

'Porgy? Why Porgy?' asked the brigadier.

'Oh, something to do with "Georgy Porgie, Pudding and Pie". I had a weakness for puddings, treacle steamed pudding in particular.'

'And for kissing girls, Mr Chairman?'

'Apple crumble, spotted dick, I loved them all,' added the chairman wistfully.

Dr Algernon Westmacott-Hill had been silent until now. 'I'd be happy to settle for Dr W-H. Five letters – only four, if we can negotiate free hyphens.'

'Enough of this.' The chairman pulled himself together and turned to the hon. treasurer. 'Trevor, I hope you have something more sensible to contribute? After all, you first drew our attention to this matter.'

The treasurer referred to his notes. 'Gentlemen, the cost of engraving names, however long, pales into insignificance in comparison with the cost of the set-up fees for sixteen trophies. We incur £204 for set-up charges before a single letter – or hyphen, come to that – has been engraved.'

'So,' said the chairman, looking puzzled, 'what can we do about that?'

'Yes,' said the brigadier, 'come on, man, spit it out!'

'I'd have thought that the answer,' said the hon. treasurer, looking rather smug, 'is to discontinue the practice of engraving trophies. The older ones dating back to the 1920s are chock-a-block with names anyway. I suggest we continue to present trophies but, instead of having them engraved, display the winner's names on a wooden honours board and mount it in the pavilion. The walls in the pavilion will provide sufficient space for honours boards for years to come.'

The treasurer sat back in his seat, confident that the merits of his lateral thinking would meet with unanimous approval. Outside, the wind whistled round the building causing the windows of the committee room to rattle ominously.

'Hang on!' said the brigadier. 'How much do these honours boards cost? Not much of a saving to be made, I'll be bound.'

'Hmm,' said the chairman looking doubtful. 'I don't think people will take kindly to having trophies without inscribed names.'

'And,' said Sir Christopher, who had enjoyed a distinguished career as an ambassador in many countries, 'after a few years I fear our modest pavilion will be overwhelmed with honours boards.'

'Well,' said the treasurer, irritated that his novel idea had not met with immediate acclaim, 'I have, of course, made some enquiries and it seems we can acquire an honours board in oak, large enough to accommodate sixteen names using comput-er-cut vinyl text, for £230. Comparing that with the cost of continuing to engrave our trophies is not entirely straightfor-ward but, if we assume an average of twenty letters for each name at 12p per letter, that gives an average cost of £2.40

per person. Multiply that by sixteen and we have a total of £38.40 for the engraving, plus the set-up fee of £204, giving an estimated grand total of £242.40. So, switching to honours boards will give a saving of approximately £12.07 per annum.'

'My dear fellow,' said the brigadier, 'just as I suspected, a ludicrously small saving. Absolutely not worth the aggro!'

Dr Algernon Westmacott-Hill, a retired brain surgeon of high repute, spoke. 'If members like me with names exceeding the average of twenty letters continue to win competitions, then Trevor's suggestion would reap greater savings. My years in the NHS taught me that every penny counts.'

'Thank you,' said the chairman. 'I suggest we put it to the vote. Those in favour of adopting honours boards?' The hon. treasurer and Dr Algernon raised their hands. 'And those against?' The brigadier and Sir Christopher raised their hands.

'It seems,' said the chairman rather wearily, 'that we do not have a consensus. I shall have to exercise my casting vote.'

The wind outside rose to a crescendo. Suddenly there was a loud explosion followed by the unmistakable sound of splintering wood.

The members of the committee rose as one and dashed to the window. There, beyond the hallowed lawns that gave so much pleasure on balmy summer days, they beheld a shocking sight. A large tree had been uprooted by the storm and fallen on the pavilion. The impact had turned the pitched roof into a grotesque V and two walls of the timber pavilion, which had stood proudly for over a hundred years, lay flat on the ground. As they watched, the wind lifted a large section of the pavilion, carried it over a yew hedge and sent it skimming into the River Thames beyond.

'Well,' said the chairman, recovering his decorum remarkably quickly, 'it seems that an Act of God has taken the decision out of our hands. Even if we wanted honours boards, we no longer have walls upon which to display them.'

No sooner had the chairman spoken than the lights in the committee room flickered and failed. The hon. treasurer, groping around in the gloom trying to gather up his precious papers, knocked a jug of orange juice over the binder containing twelve years of the club's accounts. Outside, a second chestnut tree surrendered to the storm and toppled over onto the wreckage of the sports pavilion.

The Inspirational Speaker

I'm fifty-three years of age and I was a successful inspirational speaker. You'll have noticed the past tense in that sentence: was.

I became an inspirational speaker – that's what they called me, I didn't dream it up – twenty years ago when I was thirty-three. I was never trained in public speaking, I just picked it up and people said, 'Wow! you've changed my life.' I was flabbergasted at first, but I got used to it – even began to believe the hype. True, I've always had the gift of the gab. Got me into loads of trouble at school. Always in detention for chattering. Even in detention I couldn't keep my mouth shut and that landed me in even more detentions. I left school at sixteen after taking a handful of basic GCSEs and getting mediocre grades.

Didn't have a clue what to do, so I got a job at the Outward Bound School in Cumbria. I only got the job because a pal of mine worked there looking after the equipment store. Initially I was his assistant. I used to wipe the algae off the canoes and store them on racks and sort out the mountaineering gear. I'd coil the ropes neatly and hang them on specially designed hooks. Belays and other stuff too. I liked to stand back and see everything looking tidy, helmets and waterproofs all in a row.

Anyway, one day an instructor called Geoff was short staffed and he invited me to accompany him with a group he was taking out. Sixth formers from a posh school, they'd come for the day to learn how to abseil. We went in a minibus to an outcrop of rock about five miles away. There were some girls in the group. They screamed when they went over the edge, even though I couldn't see anything really scary about it.

We were about to pack up for the day when Geoff asked me if I'd like to have a go. Couldn't believe my luck. Going over the edge backwards was great. I bounced my way down the rock face as if it were made of rubber. After that, Geoff started taking me out on other trips with other groups. Sometimes we abseiled, and sometimes we did rock climbing with ropes and all the gear. I discovered I had a natural affinity with the rocks, warm in the sun and cold at night. Sometimes we went out after dark with lights on our helmets and luminous strips on our yellow jackets. It was great.

That's how it all began, me getting hooked on rocks.

You'll have heard of the Five Peaks Challenge, here in the Lake District? Fourteen miles and five peaks conquered in one day. It's not exactly rock climbing – more rock scrambling – but it's not called a challenge for nothing. People mainly do it to raise money for charity. Anyway, after being one of the official guides for a few years, I woke up one morning and decided to see if I could do the five peaks on thirty consecutive days and have it recorded in the *Guinness Book of Records*. It just came to me as an idea and it stuck. I checked and no one else had been daft enough to try it.

The Outward Bound School were great about it. Sponsored me, let me borrow gear and gave me the month off. They wanted a share of the publicity if I succeeded. Volunteers from the mountain rescue acted as my independent witnesses, watching me set off and clocking my return.

So, twenty years ago, starting on the first of June, I set my alarm for 6am and had bacon and eggs for breakfast. Geoff drove me to Langdale and I set off at 8am. I took the usual circular route to the summit of Crinkle Crags, then on to Bow Fell, Esk Pike, Great End and, finally, Scafell Pike, England's highest mountain. A fourteen-mile up-and-down trip. Usually took me between seven and eight hours. The scenery was so familiar that I didn't waste time admiring the views, just cracked on with it. I took photos at each peak showing the date and time as evidence – 150 photos over the thirty days.

For the first week or so I'd meet a few other walkers and I'd say 'Hi', but then word got around that there was this crazy bloke doing the peaks thirty times in thirty days and well-wishers started to join me. Bit of a nuisance, really – it was much easier to stay focused when I was on my own. Sometimes people would accompany me all the way, and sometimes they'd be waiting for me at various peaks and cheer me on. I was amazed.

My gammy leg was one of the reasons why I became newsworthy. It got crushed in a road accident when I was nine. Not my fault, I got hit by a motorbike when I was crossing the road outside my house. He came round the bend too fast and I finished up being flung against a stone wall. I was in hospital for three months while they tried to fix my leg, but

I lost some muscle and it never grew properly after that. Left me with quite a limp.

On my thirtieth walk, quite a crowd accompanied me and the local press turned out to welcome me over the finishing line. There were flags and things. The Outward Bound School fêted me and invited me to give talks to groups about my adventure. It was weird to see people listening intently to my story. Some even took notes. I couldn't imagine what I'd said that was noteworthy. I used to tell them how I'd woken up one day and decided to do it and that, once I'd set my mind on it, nothing could stop me. Funny thing was, people seemed to think it was remarkable.

After a while I started getting invitations from local Rotary Clubs and even the Women's Institute. Word got around and invitations came from further afield. That's how I got to be an inspirational speaker. An agency signed me up and sent me all round the world speaking to sales teams and at conferences for business managers for a fat fee. I got to stay in posh hotels in places like Monte Carlo, Houston, Vancouver and Sydney, all expenses paid. Amazing! People kept telling me I was an inspiration and women – well, they threw themselves at me. But we won't go there.

I used to trot out some corny messages, but people lapped them up. Things like 'New day, new opportunities', 'Winners never quit', 'Aim high to hit high', 'It's your journey, no one can do it for you', 'Ambition is the road to success but persistence is what gets you there'. Short, punchy stuff delivered with apparent conviction. Can you believe people fell for stuff like that? No? Nor did I, but they did.

Then, after twenty years speaking on the circuit, without any warning I was struck dumb. Mid-sentence. No more words. Couldn't even whisper. Nothing.

At first people thought I was kidding. I was flown home for tests. Saw lots of specialists. They thought I must have had some sort of stroke but nothing showed up on the brain scans.

Eventually I was sent to a speech therapist. She told me she'd read of other cases where people suddenly ran out of words. The condition had a fancy Latin name – *glossarium interruptum*, or something like that. She said the theory was that everyone was born with an undisclosed word quota and that I'd used up mine. Apparently people who talk a lot are at risk – stand-up comedians, teachers and politicians, for example.

I'm keeping this brief because I've been warned there might also be a quota for written words, not just spoken ones. I really hope that's not...

The Journal

This is weird. Hang on – I wonder if that's a fact or a feeling? It certainly *feels* weird so I guess it's a feeling. But if it feels weird, doesn't that make it a fact as far as I'm concerned? But if it's a fact for me but not for anyone else, surely it's just a feeling? Oh hell, I knew I'd get myself tied up in knots.

Still, as a colleague at work used to say, 'If you don't start, you don't start.' Profound, eh? So here I am with the notebook I've bought specially from Rymans open at the first page. I expect it's obvious that I'm feeling a bit uncertain about how to proceed. Ah, 'feeling uncertain' – that's another feeling, isn't it? Need to flag them up.

Perhaps I'd feel better if I drew a margin down the right-hand side of each page like we used to do at school? And put the date? A bit of displacement activity never did anybody any harm. I know I'm supposed to relax and let it all hang out, but I'm not really sure how to do that, hence all this rambling. You see, Dr Jackson, I've never been asked to do anything like keep a journal before. Still, you're the therapist. Anything to keep you happy!

Truth is, I'm a placid, easy-going sort of person not at all given to introspection. My philosophy is simple: keep cheerful and get on with things. Yep, I'm a great believer in keeping busy. I find it's therapeutic. But I have to admit something's amiss, otherwise why would I keep getting these blasted headaches like having my head squeezed in a vice? At first I thought I might need new specs, but I went to the optician and my prescription hadn't changed.

No, thinking back I'm pretty sure they started when things got a bit fraught at work. The trouble is I hate confrontation, so I didn't complain when my new boss started overloading me with extra work. I've never had a woman as a boss before and, I admit, I was a bit thrown. She was American too. Rather brash. Used to say things like 'that's about as useful as tits on a bull' and 'let's get to where the rubber hits the road'. Made me wince. She swore a lot, too.

Anyway, when she started to give me stuff to do with impossible deadlines, I buckled down and got on with it as best I could. As a consequence, I became seriously overloaded and everything got on top of me. I knew I should be upfront and tell her I wasn't coping, but I didn't. I just kowtowed and the resentment started building up. Hey, there's another feeling: resentment.

Things eventually resolved themselves when my boss came a cropper. She lost her cool, sacked someone on the spot and was taken to a tribunal for wrongful dismissal. The judgement went against her and she finished up getting sacked. Quite a relief! But my headaches persisted. It was as if they'd become a habit. The least thing would set them off: misplacing things, cutting it fine when catching a train, my laptop playing up.

My forehead even started tingling the other day when I was wondering which pocket to put things in. I'd got used to trousers with two bum pockets and I was completely thrown when I discovered I'd accidentally bought trousers with only one pocket at the back. Completely mucked up my usual routine. Pathetic, eh?

My headaches have definitely got worse since my wife announced that she wants to move to a smaller, more manageable house. She didn't actually use the word 'downsizing', but that's what it amounts to. It would be a nightmare for me, though not for Susan – she's totally organised and doesn't hang on to things. But lots of my stuff would have to go, it certainly couldn't be accommodated in a smaller house. The very thought fills me with the screaming heebie-jeebies. Wow, there's a feeling: the screaming heebie-jeebies! On a scale of one to ten, one being a doddle and ten a disaster, the prospect of moving house is a definite nine, maybe even a borderline ten.

That's enough scribbling for today. Just writing all this stuff has brought on a blasted headache. I'll do more tomorrow.

Me again. As usual, my headache wore off after a night's sleep, even though I dreamt that a removal lorry arrived before I'd had time to sort anything. I looked out of the window and there it was. Four big blokes were clambering out, eyeing up the house and rubbing their hands with glee. Even if I've had a disturbed night, my headache is never there first thing in the morning. It comes on gradually as the day takes its toll.

Anyway, as I was saying, I dread the idea of moving house. It definitely gives me a problem. Is a problem a feeling? I suppose if it feels like a problem, it must be one. Someone once told me that a problem is a gap, the difference between what you've got and what you want. Well, this gap feels like a bloody great chasm!

It's okay for Susan because she's organised and tidy. My trouble is that I've kept things when I should have ditched them or, I suppose, not acquired them in the first place. Truth is, I had the space for self-indulgence and I convinced myself that the treasures I've collected might, just might, come in useful one day. Maybe even be worth something.

Well, to be honest (honest? this journal has a lot to answer for!) that's not quite true. As Susan often reminds me, I've got lots of things that are never, ever going to be useful or that anyone is likely to want. My collection of car wheel hubs, for example, and all the right- handed gloves I've found left accidentally on trains or displayed on railings.

Another example would be my rusty rivets – six of them – picked up (I suppose stolen might be more accurate) when I visited SS *Great Britain* soon after it had arrived back in Bristol after being towed on a raft all the way from the Falkland Isles. There were lots of them in heaps on the floor of the dry dock. I've often wondered how puzzled the restorers must have been when they discovered six rivets, possibly once admired by the great Isambard Kingdom Brunel himself, were missing.

And then there is the cobblestone from Paris, scooped into my rucksack when I happened to find some unattended road works near the Arc de Triomphe. It's a whitish cube, looks as if it might even be marble, dressed on five sides so that it would fit snugly in place, like a piece in a jigsaw. I like to think the entourage carrying Napoleon's remains passed over my cobblestone on their way to Les Invalides.

I've seen programmes on TV where cheerful presenters have

ruthlessly decluttered a house that's become an absolute tip. Watching, I've always felt a touch smug because my things certainly aren't clutter. In any case, our house has always been tidy. You see, Susan is houseproud and the parts of the house under her jurisdiction are pristine. To locate my stuff you'd have to pry: open cupboards, clamber up a ladder, peer into the loft. Or descend into the cellar. Oh, and look in the garage that our car has never occupied. Fortunately, none of our visitors ever venture into these places so my precious possessions have remained undetected by the outside world. Susan knows about them of course, but that doesn't count. Anyway, until the prospect of downsizing reared its ugly head, she has always been tolerant, even mildly amused by my collections.

My headache is back again! Just the thought of having to decide what to keep and what to dispose of brings it on. Take my vast collection of bottles, both glass and plastic. Some of the plastic ones claim to be recyclable and some of them boast that they are 'proudly made from 50% recycled PET'. The fact is that by storing them I'm helping to save the planet. I'm reducing noise pollution, too. If you live near a pub (we do, that's where most of my bottles come from) you'll have heard the excruciating noise as hundreds of empty glass bottles cascade into the back of a refuse truck.

I've even got some Victorian bottles, retrieved from a nearby building site when the foundations were being dug. The workmen didn't care, they carried on digging trenches with their bulldozers, dumping the soil in big heaps with the poor bottles ruthlessly exposed, blinking in the sunlight. I used to go each evening and rescue them. There was a place where I could squeeze in through the temporary fence that sported 'keep out' notices. I've got quite a good collection, most of them green but some brown and some a delightful blue.

You might wonder why I'm in such a stew about having to ditch some of my treasures. My homespun theory is that it's because, when I was a kid (I was an army brat), my parents moved house seven times (just totted it up). Every time my stuff got ditched: my comic collection; the brass bullet casings I'd found on a firing range; the fragments of Roman pottery I'd dug out of a disused quarry; the samples I'd been given on a school trip to a blanket factory, even the cigarette cards I'd collected of footballers and wayside flowers. I was never into stamps, but I guess they'd have gone the same way. So basically, it's all to do with loss. Might that explain why I'm getting in a tizz?

That's quite enough rambling for today. I know I must pull myself together and stop procrastinating so I'm off to the cellar to make a start on the basis that if you don't start, you don't start (have I said that before?). More tomorrow.

***

Hello, Dr Jackson, Susan here. Unfortunately, Brian can't continue with his journal because he's had a nasty accident. Yesterday he was mucking about in the cellar – I'm not sure exactly what he was doing – when the shelf where he stacked his collection of *Men Only* magazines (I don't suppose he told you about his magazines?) collapsed under the weight and knocked him over. He fell awkwardly, landing sideways on some of his precious bottles. He was badly cut – shards of broken glass pierced a lung and narrowly missed one of his kidneys. Anyway, he has had extensive surgery and is recovering in hospital.

Of course, Brian's accident will temporarily halt preparations to put our house on the market. I'm tempted to get people in to clear his clutter. I've seen a programme on the telly, I think it's called *Big House Clear Out*. I wonder if I they'd take it on.

I'm afraid Brian's likely to be out of action for a while, but I'm sure he'll be in touch to arrange another appointment once he's home again. In the meantime, I'm popping these pages in the post to you.

The Letters

Most daughters love their mother but I hated mine. It was a great relief when she died, aged only sixty-seven, killed by a lifetime puffing away on fags. My husband, Paul, was convinced I'd be stricken with remorse or guilt but I was cock-a-hoop. No more dutiful monthly visits. No more sitting there wondering how an hour could pass so slowly. No more pretending not to notice the faint pong of urine. No more small talk and suppressing the urge to rise to her snide remarks. No more listening to her grumbling about the callousness of the nursing-home staff. Bliss.

I behaved myself at her funeral, looking suitably sombre, but inside I was saying 'yippee'! Apart, that is, from feeling frustrated by some unfinished business.

My mother's name was Mabel. When she could no longer breathe without the aid of an oxygen cylinder on a purpose-built trolley, we insisted that she'd have to go into a nursing home. We had to sell her house to raise money to pay the fees. She was totally against the sale, harbouring the delusion that she'd recover sufficiently to be able to return to independent living.

Paul found the suitcase in the loft when we were clearing Mabel's house. Looking in the loft had been an afterthought. We'd been visiting the house for years but the loft had never been mentioned. The garden shed, the garage, the tumbledown conservatory had all featured in conversations from time to time, but the loft – never.

It only occurred to me that we should check the loft after the man in a white van had cleared the house of all its furniture. He gave us £350 for the lot and drove away with a grin on his face. We'd already filled our Volvo to the roof with knick-knacks: Toby jugs and vases from various mantelpieces; silver candlesticks and a bone-china tea set from the dresser in the dining room; cut-glass decanters from the corner cupboard in the sitting room; some silver photo frames from occasional tables; Mabel's dressing table set from her bedroom; family photo albums from the games cupboard; books; a walking stick with a carved bone handle, and the silver cigarette case given to my stepfather as a retirement present.

Paul and I wandered round the empty house feeling like vandals, remembering how the rooms had looked before they were stripped bare. 'Should we check the loft?' I asked, looking at the hatch high up in the landing ceiling.

'Nothing to stand on and I can't reach it,' said Paul. 'We'd need a stepladder.'

'The next door neighbours are sure to have one,' I suggested. Rather reluctantly, Paul went to ask if we might borrow a stepladder.

Mabel's loft was unremarkable – dark and dusty, the only light provided by a single low-watt bulb. Paul could make out some cardboard boxes and bundles of unused insulation fibre in the gloom. One box turned out to be full of abandoned curtains, another with pairs of old shoes. Some faded piano music lay between the joists, and Paul found a small brown suitcase covered in dust over by the cold-water tank.

'Hey, Jen, better check this out,' he said, handing the case down to me through the open hatch.

I sneezed and tried the rusty catches. They wouldn't budge. 'I can't open it,' I called up. 'We'll take it home with the rest of the stuff.'

Only after I had married Paul and had children of my own was I able to admit that I hated my mother. She was a selfish, egotistical witch! Her first husband, my father, had been killed in the last few weeks of WW2. I was only a toddler and have no memory of him. A couple of years later my mother remarried. I used to wonder what would happen if my father came back and found my mother with another man. Whenever I asked about my real father, she would burst into tears and tell me I was cruel to upset her.

After my mother married again, I was sent away to a boarding school. I was only seven. The school was run by nuns who enforced a strict regime. I was very unhappy and begged my mother to take me away. I once climbed a large tree in the grounds and sat up there all day, refusing to come down. On another occasion I ran away, but I had nowhere to go. The police found me wandering aimlessly around the country lanes and took me back.

Eventually I was expelled, only to be sent to another boarding school where the music teacher used to abuse me during piano lessons. I once made the mistake of telling my mother what was happening. She was sitting at her dressing table putting on her makeup. She lit a cigarette and said, 'Don't be silly, dear. Let's talk about it later.' The subject was never raised again.

My stepfather was besotted with my mother. He was a career diplomat with a succession of overseas postings. Sometimes I was flown out to join them during school holidays, but more often than not I stayed with my granny in Devon. She was caring and cuddly, but she worried about money and often grumbled that my parents hadn't sent anything towards my keep.

Whenever I stayed with my parents, I felt as if I were intruding. My stepfather generally treated me well, but I was always conscious that he wasn't my real father. Once, when I was a teenager, he dropped me off at a friend's birthday party. I was feeling self-conscious, all dressed up in a pretty dress and wearing some lipstick. As I got out of the car my stepfather suddenly said, 'You'll never be as good looking as your mother, you know.' I was totally deflated but I knew he was right. Before she became ill, my mother had film-star looks.

Paul used a small hacksaw to cut through the catches on the case. It was full of dog-eared envelopes stacked vertically in bundles. Each bundle was tied with ribbon and each envelope was numbered in the bottom left-hand corner.

I opened the first envelope and started to read. It was dated 4 February 1942, and had been written by my father from an army base on the south coast. More letters followed – lots of them. I sat entranced, reading letters written by the father I had never known. Normally I'd feel sneaky reading someone else's letters, but not this time: I felt utterly entitled.

The first bundle of letters had been sent from various army camps in the UK. They were followed by two-years' worth of airmail envelopes from India and Burma. The letters, written on flimsy paper with many redacted passages, described the harsh conditions endured in the jungle fighting the Japanese. At the end of March 1945 the letters stopped abruptly, to be followed by a telegram, conspicuous in its yellow envelope, reporting that my father was missing in action. The telegram was followed by letters from the War Office confirming that my father had almost certainly been killed.

Next in the sequence was a handwritten letter from my father's commanding officer, expressing his condolences and giving an account of what had happened. The colonel described how my father had been leading a patrol that was ambushed by Japanese soldiers. After a brief gun battle, my father was seen to fall to the ground. The rest of the patrol made it back to camp. The next day a search party was sent out but they found no trace of my father's body.

There was also a letter from the army padre, a Major Maurice Garnett, saying what a popular fellow my father had been and that a makeshift memorial service, held one evening at the jungle HQ, had been well attended.

I read the letters compulsively with tears rolling down my cheeks. Paul comforted me and read them too. 'Well, at least you now know what happened to your father.'

'Yes, but the letters are inconclusive. They never confirm that he was definitely killed, only that he was missing in action, presumed dead.'

There were more letters. The next bundle contained passionate letters written by my stepfather, begging Mabel to marry him. After they were married, there were letters written from various foreign embassies saying how he longed to be reunited with Mabel. They included racy descriptions of what he wanted to do with her; sometimes, for the avoidance of any doubt, there were explicit sketches. His letters stopped abruptly when, after fifteen years of apparent marital bliss, he went into hospital and died from complications after contracting a rare tropical disease.

Amazingly, after a suitable interval, the love letters resumed. This time they were written by two different admirers, apparently unaware of each other's existence, both imploring Mabel to marry them.

I made two decisions. The first was that, now I knew my father's army number, I would visit the Army Museum to see if I could find out more. The second decision was that I wouldn't mention the letters to my mother whilst I did some investigating. It was hard to believe she'd forgotten about them. She could remember the exact location of various knick-knacks, often asking us to bring in a particular vase or silver photo frame, so surely she couldn't have forgotten about the suitcase in the loft.

They were helpful at the Army Museum but puzzled that they could trace no record of my father's death being officially confirmed. It was a mystery. I continued to visit my mother, feeling smug that I'd read her letters and, in a perverse way, enjoying making no mention of them. I'd look at her and think, *You cow! I begged you to tell me about my father. You could easily have let me read his letters years ago. Now you can damn well wait until I'm ready to tell you I've found them.*

Then, a few months after I'd found them, Mabel suddenly asked, 'Have you got a small suitcase full of letters?'

I was tempted to say 'I thought you'd never bloody well ask', but I replied calmly, 'Yes, Paul found the suitcase in the loft.

Do you want me to bring the letters in?'

'Yes, dear, that would be nice. I'd like to read them again.'

Before my next visit I retrieved the suitcase from the top of the wardrobe where I'd left it. The case, now with no latches, would no longer close, so I transferred the bundles of letters into a cardboard shoe box. They fitted snugly.

The lining on the bottom of the empty suitcase was frayed. Tucked away inside, I found another letter. The postmark was dated 1949 and, even though my mother had remarried two years previously, it was addressed to her using my father's surname: Mrs Mabel Pickard.

I opened the envelope with trembling fingers. Why had it had been hidden? The letter was from Maurice Garnett, my father's army padre.

Dear Mrs Pickard

I appreciate that this letter may be distressing, but I thought it right to inform you that your husband, Captain Robert Pickard, may be alive. Reports have been received that a man fitting his description is living in a remote village in Burma. Apparently the villagers have adopted him as one of their own but he refuses to answer any questions or to confirm his identity. When approached, he runs away and hides in the jungle.

In the meantime, the authorities are doing their best to establish his identity and you may well receive official notification of this from the War Office.

I appreciate that, having been told your husband was almost certainly killed in March 1945, news that he may have survived will be unsettling to say the least. Please be assured that I will do all I can to help.

As you see, I'm now based at Chelsea Barracks and my contact details are above. Please feel free to telephone me. It would be good to have a chat even though, for the time being, details of your husband's whereabouts remain far from certain.

Most sincerely
Maurice Garnett
Major, RAChD.

Utterly flabbergasted, I read the letter again and again. Why had my mother hidden it? Had she contacted Garnett as he had suggested? If so, what had he been able to tell her? Had my father been identified? Had he been repatriated to the UK? What had become of him? I ripped the tattered lining out of the empty case, but there were no more letters.

Paul came home from work. 'Jen, this is outrageous! You've a perfect right to know what happened to your father. You'll have to confront your mother and demand an explanation.'

'I wonder if Garnett is still alive,' I said.

We searched online; in *Crockford's Clerical Directory*, we found a Canon Maurice Garnett, retired, living in Andover in Hampshire.

'That's almost certainly him,' said Paul. 'He must be well into his eighties by now. Why not write to him, Jen?'

I needed no encouragement.

Dear Canon Garnett

I am hoping you can help me solve a mystery. I have found a letter you wrote in 1949 to my mother, Mrs Mabel Pickard, about my father, Captain Robert Pickard, who was presumed to have

been killed in action in Burma in March 1945. In your letter,
which I have only recently found, you say there were reports that
Captain Pickard might have survived and be living with villagers
in the Burmese jungle.

I will quite understand if you have no memory of writing to
my mother, but I am naturally curious to know whether she ever
contacted you, as you kindly suggested she might, and whether you
ever received any more news of my father.

Please let me know if you can help and forgive me for disturbing
your retirement. My telephone number, should you wish to phone,
is 020 7973 229050.

Yours sincerely
Jennifer Smeaton

Two days later my phone rang.

'Maurice Garnett here, Mrs Smeaton.' He cleared his throat; his voice sounded old. 'I was pleased to get your letter, and I do remember writing to your mother all those years ago. Unfortunately I didn't get a reply. I've often wondered if she ever received it.'

'You never heard from my mother?'

'No, nothing, I'm afraid. I believe the War Office wrote to her, too, but got no response.'

'How extraordinary! Did you ever learn more about what happened to my father?'

'Unfortunately not. He was sighted a number of times in the years after the war, but he clearly wished to conceal his identity and eventually vanished and was never seen again. The villagers were questioned by the authorities, but it was all very vague. All they'd say was that one day he packed up and left to travel further north. They assumed he'd gone to live in another village.'

'So no one knows what became of him?'

'I'm afraid not, Mrs Smeaton. It was most unsatisfactory. I'm sorry I can't be more helpful.'

After the call, I sat for a long time wondering what to do next: give my mother the shoebox full of letters and say nothing? Confront her with the letter from Maurice Garnett and demand an explanation? Ask if she had ever replied and, if not, why not? Ask her why she had always refused to tell me anything about my father? Ask if my stepfather knew about Garnett's letter and the rumours that my father may have survived the war? The questions were endless.

I resolved to confront my mother and to hell with upsetting her. I put on my coat, picked up the shoebox and took the car keys off the hook in the kitchen. The phone rang. I thought perhaps it might be Canon Garnett ringing back having recalled something further.

'Mrs Smeaton, it's the nursing home. I don't want to upset you, but please come as soon as you can. Your mother has slipped into unconsciousness and, according to your wishes, there are no plans to resuscitate her.'

I sat by her bed wondering whether, if she opened her eyes, I'd have the nerve to ask any of my questions. Her mouth hung open and her shallow breathing petered out in the early hours of the morning.

On my mother's bedside table, almost within her reach, was the shoebox full of love letters.

The Nine-Day Wonder

She was besotted with her latest acquisition. None of her other possessions could compete: not her jewels, not her collection of Jimmy Choo shoes, not the designer clothes and handbags in her large walk-in wardrobe – not even her new lover.

Jessica had never needed to write a CV, but if she had it would have been brief:

Left school with no plans. At age eighteen, joined a successful advertising agency as a general dogsbody. Worked my way up to becoming the owner's PA. At twenty-six, married him. At twenty-eight, widowed (husband perished in a helicopter crash). Inherited everything. Never looked back.

Now aged thirty-two, with a mews house near Harrods, a country pile in Hampshire and a holiday cottage in Cumbria, not to mention sole ownership of a thriving advertising agency employing fifty talented people, Jessica lived a carefree, hedonistic existence.

'What ya doing today?' enquired Matt over a leisurely breakfast, whilst flicking through the pages of *Plumbing Weekly*.

'Hmm, not sure.' Jessica adjusted her silk dressing gown which, though comfortable against her skin, had a tendency to slip open. 'I think I'll buy a new car.'

'A new car? Shit, you've got four already.'

Jessica chose to ignore the implication that four were sufficient. 'Yes, but I've seen one I really fancy. Jeremy Clarkson gave it a five star-rating.'

'Oh? What is it?' Matt gazed at her over his magazine. She loved his doleful, dark-brown eyes. They reminded her of how, when she was a teenager, her pet Labrador used to look longingly up at her when he wanted a walk.

'None of your business.' She knew he didn't really care.

Jessica did everything on a whim as the mood took her, and Matt was a case in point. He had come to quote for the installation of a new en-suite bathroom which, needless to say, could only be reached via the main bedroom with its generous four-poster bed. As he busied himself taking photos on his mobile and measuring this and that, she'd dallied, enjoying his broad shoulders and bulging biceps. She'd wondered how far his tattoos extended beneath his jeans and shirt.

Now, six weeks later, both the en suite and Matt were fully functioning installations, though, if history repeated itself, Jessica knew the former would definitely outlast the latter.

Jessica lay back in her huge cast-iron bath, resplendent on its ball-and-claw feet, her buxom body submerged beneath a generous carpet of bubbles. She knew she should do something about her weight but she enjoyed Matt, lithe and muscular with a six pack he could ripple, exploring her curves and crevices. She resolved to take herself in hand post-Matt, whenever that might be. She gave a contented sigh, turned on the gold tap with her big toe and topped up the hot water.

Back in her dressing gown, Jessica phoned her office. On days when she didn't put in an appearance, she was in the habit of getting an update from the general manager, a competent man on whom she increasingly relied. He assured her all was well and told her that McLaren, the F1 team, had invited them to tender for a lucrative advertising contract. She entered the time and date for the presentation in her electronic diary. She excelled at pitching for new business, shamelessly flaunting herself before groups of mainly male company directors.

Smiling to herself, Jessica took her laptop outside and sat under the parasol by her swimming pool. She clicked on the Top Gear website and reread the opening words of the review: *'A real supercar, there's nothing to compete. Even when parked, it looks like it's having fun. Don't over-think it. Just do it.'*

Don't over-think it. She loved that advice, wise words that perfectly summed up her philosophy of life. She'd have them printed on a T-shirt – far more profound than the one she often wore with the words *'All this and brains too!'* emblazoned across her ample bosom.

She searched for the nearest dealership and watched a video, drooling over the images: the sleek wedge shape; the doors that opened like a bird of prey taking flight; the massive air intakes reminiscent of a Harrier jet; the obscene exhausts and the vulgar spoiler; the black aluminium wheels with bright-yellow brake pads; the stitched leather seats; the array of electronics in the cockpit...

It was drop-dead gorgeous. She *had* to have it! Jessica picked up her mobile and phoned the dealer's number. After three electronic rings a voice said, 'Good morning. You're through to Adam. How may I help you?'

'Thank you. It's your lucky day. I want to buy one of the cars in your showroom.'

'Certainly madam. Which one?'

'The Lamborghini.'

There was a pause. 'The Lamborghini? Are you sure?'

'Of course I'm sure. The purple one with yellow brake pads.'

'You mean the Aventador with the V12 engine? You say you want to *buy* it?'

'Yes, I want to buy it. I want it delivered this afternoon.'

'Delivered? For a test drive?'

'Never mind a test drive, I want to buy it. A cash sale. What's your best offer?'

'A cash sale?' The voice sounded incredulous.

'For God's sake, stop repeating everything I say! Put me through to your manager.'

'My manager?'

'Yes, your bloody manager. Now, pronto!'

'May I have your name?'

'Jessica Slaughter. Now put me through to your manager.'

The phone fell silent. Jessica waited, feeling increasingly aggravated. She was temperamentally unsuited to waiting.

'Hello,' said a new smarmy voice. 'Maurice speaking. I understand you are enquiring about the Lamborghini Aventador?'

'No, I'm not enquiring. I want to buy it.'

'You want to *buy* it?'

'Yes,' screamed Jessica. 'I want to buy the bloody thing! Right now. Today!'

Long before it came into sight, Jessica heard the guttural roar of the car's vast engine. Even when it had turned into the drive, it clung low to the ground and could only be glimpsed as it passed the occasional gap in the yew hedges. An online transfer of £449,950 had finally convinced Maurice that she was serious.

The car drew to a halt, the engine fell silent, the doors raised up magically and Maurice emerged, looking sheepish but clutching a bottle of Champagne and a huge bunch of flowers. 'Apologies for the misunderstanding, Ms Slaughter. We usually only sell these to Arabs or Russian oligarchs. I've never known a woman buy one before.'

'That's as may be,' snorted Jessica, enjoying his discomfort.

She signed the paperwork, took delivery of the instruction manual with pages of incomprehensible technical data, and declined his offer to take her for a familiarisation run.

'Wow!' Matt exclaimed when he came home. 'You said you were going to buy a car, not a fuckin' Lamborghini. Are you sure you can handle it?'

Uncharacteristically, Jessica bit her tongue.

The next day, after Matt had left in his white van with its collection of toilets and hand basins, Jessica parked the Lamborghini on the lawn so that she could admire its flowing lines whilst sitting by the pool. She opened the leather-bound manual and read and re-read the introduction:

Giving a glimpse of the future today, revolutionary thinking is at the heart of every Lamborghini. Whether it is the aerospace-inspired design, or the technologies applied to the V12 engine, or the carbon-fibre structure, going beyond accepted limits is part of our philosophy. Your Aventador, coming from a family of supercars already considered legendary, advances every concept of performance, establishing itself as the benchmark for super-sports cars.

Each and every detail of your Aventador, crafted by skilled artisans, bears the hallmarks of the House of the Raging Bull. It is a true masterpiece of design that expresses dynamism and power, with an interior that combines high-level technology and luxury equipment.

Jessica paused, adjusted her sunglasses and leaned back on her sun lounger. Like an actress learning her lines, she mouthed, 'A glimpse of the future today ... a benchmark ... crafted by skilled artisans ... a masterpiece of design.'

She roused herself and walked over to the car, shimmering in the morning sunlight. She circled it slowly, like a lioness sizing up her prey, then she lay flat on the grass, gazing in wonder at the huge chrome exhaust pipes. After a while, she got up, brushed herself down, and pressed her fob to open the doors. She watched them swing up obediently. Then she closed them and did it again and again, just for the hell of it.

She lowered herself into the cockpit, the crafted driving seat hugging her body, and ran her eyes over the array of instruments. She started the engine, engaged a gear and the car crept forward. She opted to drive slowly along the country lanes, her foot resting lightly on the accelerator, relishing the throb of the engine and perversely enjoying its subjugation.

The day for the presentation to the McLaren management team arrived. Jessica rose early, bathed, carefully arranged her hair, did her make-up and squeezed herself into a designer dress that showed off her curves.

'Blimey, you've scrubbed up well. Going somewhere?' Matt asked at breakfast.

'Yep. McLaren.'

'What car ya taking?'

'The Lamborghini, of course. Should make a good impression.'

'Not the gold Merc?'

'Nope. Definitely the Lamborghini.'

The drive to the McLaren Technology Centre was uneventful. Jessica chose to drive in the slow lane, amused at the honks and thumbs-up that overtaking motorists gave her. She arrived in good time and parked in a lay-by to check her mascara and redo her lipstick.

As she approached the impressive building, a security guard leapt out and guided her to a parking place nearest to the front door. She opened the wing doors, slipped on her high heels and, with some difficulty, hauled herself upright out of the cockpit. She checked in at the reception desk, was issued with a visitor's pass and handed in her key fob.

The presentation went well and Jessica was pleased to see the all-male audience gazing at her more often than looking at the PowerPoints. They laughed at her jokes and nodded approvingly when she answered their questions. The marketing director wound up the event by thanking Jessica profusely and inviting her to lunch in the management dining room.

Jessica flirted shamelessly with her escort throughout the meal and, when it was over, he leaned forward over his coffee to whisper conspiratorially that the advertising contract was 'in the bag'.

Three hours later, back at reception, Jessica surrendered her visitor's pass and asked for her fob. The receptionist looked puzzled and asked Jessica to wait while a phone call was made. Shortly afterwards, a man Jessica hadn't seen before arrived looking flustered.

'Am I to understand the Lamborghini was yours?'

'Yep. Where's my fob?'

'I'm afraid there's been a mix-up.'

'A mix-up?'

Yes, your car has gone to the stripping lab.'

'The stripping lab?'

'Yes, I'm so sorry. Your car is in pieces. We mistook it for the Aventador we had ordered.' He added, as if it were an adequate explanation, 'We learn so much from stripping down competitors' models.'

Jessica returned home in a chauffeur-driven car, courtesy of McLaren, with the advertising contract signed and sealed and a cheque for £449,950 in her handbag.

'Where's the Lamborghini?' Matt smirked. 'Written it off already?'

Jessica didn't hesitate. She made an irreversible 'don't overthink it' decision: it was curtains for Matt and curtains for supercars.

The Obsession

He was the last person you'd suspect of having itchy fingers. Having led a blameless life, a yellow skip outside the pub a mile or so from the vicarage unexpectedly unsettled him.

The Reverend William Stenning, affectionately nicknamed Father Bill by his flock, was a large rotund man in his late fifties, bald, with a kindly face and twinkling eyes. At a recent jumble sale, a couple of parishioners running the second-hand bookstall had showed him a picture of Friar Tuck claiming it looked exactly like him. Grudgingly, he had to admit that there was a remarkable likeness.

He had first spotted the skip when passing it in his Volvo estate on his way to administer the last rites to a parishioner who was fading away at home, his wife holding his limp hand. Despite looking steadfastly at the road ahead, he caught a fleeting glimpse of the skip in his peripheral vision. He saw what he thought were chair legs pointed skywards like synchronised swimmers. He resolved to take a more careful look on his return journey.

He was familiar with the Red Lion, sometimes calling in to

get a bottle of gin for his wife. As a non-drinker himself, he always felt uncomfortable in the pub. He worried that people might think he was the gin drinker rather than his wife, and he was aware of cheerful banter petering out as soon as he stepped over the threshold. He'd leave as quickly as he could, clutching a gin bottle wrapped in a twist of blue paper, and hear the hubbub resume as soon as he closed the front door. He imagined jokes being made at his expense.

Everyone in the village had been taken by surprise when, in his early fifties, Father Bill had married the churchwarden's widow, a slight, bird-like woman five years his senior. Her late husband had fallen on hard times after losing all his money in a Lloyd's syndicate. People assumed that Father Bill, up until then a confirmed bachelor, had felt sorry for her.

She loved a tipple (or two or three) after a tedious day of secretarial work at the Oxfam offices in the nearby town, reasoning that she deserved a drink – indeed had *earned* a drink – by going out to work to supplement Father Bill's meagre stipend. On her return, she'd kick off her shoes and don a thick dressing gown and fluffy slippers. The Victorian vicarage was chilly even on balmy summer days, and in the winter the central heating was only ever fired up on special occasions when, for example, the deacon came to lunch.

On his return journey, Father Bill slowed right down as he passed the Red Lion. The skip occupied one of the parking bays in a corner of the pub's small car park. The chair legs still protruded and he calculated they must be attached to at least four chairs, with more possibly lingering unseen in the bowels of the skip.

He was still wearing his dog collar and cassock and resisted the temptation to stop and conduct a closer inspection. He considered it would be undignified for him to be caught loitering near a skip, particularly loitering with what could be construed as intent. Steve, the publican, might spot him or, worse still, Mavis, Steve's buxom, chatterbox wife.

Father Bill returned to the vicarage, made himself a cup of instant coffee and retired to his study to compose the following Sunday's sermon. He had acquired a well-earned reputation as a popular preacher, mainly because of his self-imposed rule that no sermon should last more than ten minutes. Having been a priest for nearly thirty-five years, he had become accustomed to recycling previous sermons. He kept them, written in his own hand on Basildon Bond notepaper, in the bottom drawer of his rolltop desk. However, a couple of years ago on his return from an exchange holiday (he had swapped parishes for a month with a vicar in the Lake District), he had opened the drawer to discover a family of mice nesting cosily in a confetti of shredded sermons. He assumed this was a sign that the good Lord was admonishing his laziness and urging him to produce new material.

But he couldn't concentrate; the discarded chairs lingered stubbornly in his mind's eye, distracting him from more pressing tasks such as composing Sunday's sermon on the theme of 'thou shalt not steal' (he hoped it would strengthen his resolve!), writing an overdue cheque for the butcher and changing the light bulb in his wife's bedside lamp. Anyway, he told himself, he didn't even need more chairs – except perhaps to add to the motley collection in the village hall. It seemed wrong to let them go to a landfill when, if not too rickety, they could be put to good use.

He decided, as he so often did when wracked with inde-cision, to procrastinate. He would postpone doing anything about the skip for two whole days, giving time, he reasoned, for fate to intervene. If the skip was still there, it would be a sign (presumably from above) that the chairs were Meant To Be.

Avoiding the pub for two days proved tricky. His wife suddenly announced that she needed more gin but, without telling her, he used the small end of the measure to eke out the supply. Furthermore, reaching the church and the western half of his parish without passing the pub meant he had to take a circuitous route. Inconvenient though this was, he convinced himself it would be cheating to check up on the skip during its allotted time in purdah.

Two long days passed. On the third day he rose, conscious that the pub car park beckoned. He shaved slowly, feeling a mixture of apprehension and excitement. As he gazed in the mirror, he urged himself to keep calm. After breakfast, his wife left for work and the vicarage fell silent. He deliberately dallied, washing up the breakfast dishes, making the bed, vacuuming the sitting room, winding up the wall clock in his study – a leaving present from the grateful congregation of his last parish.

The day was fine and he decided to forego the Volvo and walk to the Red Lion, hoping – indeed praying – that he'd find an empty space where the skip had been. He turned the final bend and, as he drew level with the car park, closed his eyes, counted slowly to ten then suddenly opened them. His heart sank: the cursed thing was still there, its yellow sides glistening mockingly in the morning sunshine. In an instant he was plunged back into a state of dissonance.

That evening, having long maintained that a problem shared

was a problem halved, he told his wife about his quandary over the chairs.

'But why do you want them, dear?' she asked, sipping her G&T. 'We don't need any more chairs.'

'It's not a question of *wanting* them,' he replied, somewhat exasperated. 'More a question of *saving* them.'

'Saving them? They're chairs, they don't have souls,' she chuckled.

'Saving them from landfill,' snorted Father Bill, irritated by his wife's lack of empathy.

The next day, after a restless night dreaming about approaching a skip that suddenly snarled and snapped shut, he returned to the car park sporting a pair of binoculars. He had dressed casually hoping that, if challenged, claiming he was bird watching would seem a plausible explanation for his presence.

His aim, if he could remember how to focus the binoculars, was to ascertain how many chairs the skip contained. He climbed a low stile over the wall opposite the pub and huffed and puffed up an incline in the field beyond. The top of the field provided an admirable vantage point. Having caught his breath, he trained the binoculars on the skip and counted the chair legs. There were six chairs, possibly eight, not just four as he had previously reckoned.

He returned to the vicarage and the sanctity of his study to ponder his options. Never one to make hasty decisions, he was well-practised in pondering. His decision to marry late in life had not been taken lightly. Far from it; he had compiled a list of pros and cons, adding to it over the course of many days. On balance, he thought it a good idea to marry for companionship as he grew older, but for a few days the cons equalled the pros and the decision hung in the balance.

Thankfully the impasse was broken when, on his knees in his church asking for guidance, the leading contender (his parish was awash with eligible widows) miraculously appeared cradling lilies in her arms. She apologised for disturbing him and explained that it was her turn to do the flowers in the chancel. Confident that his prayers had been answered and still on his knees, Father Bill proposed on the spot.

So, what should he do about the chairs? He made a list – he loved lists, a harmless displacement activity that postponed action and gave him the illusion of being purposeful.

1. Forget the chairs.

2. Ask Steve if he could have them.

3. Fold down the back seat in the Volvo estate and go and get them.

He paused. Number 1 had thus far proved elusive. Number 2 would be demeaning; he hadn't warmed to Steve, the publican, and would have to swallow his pride. Number 3 was perilous. What if he, a man of the cloth, was caught red-handed, trespassing and stealing from a skip? The indignity of it. Steve's wife, Mavis, the chatterbox, would make sure he never lived it down. Perhaps the answer was to do the deed at the dead of night, maybe wearing a disguise, but to be exposed in the unforgiving glare of security lights would be doubly embarrassing. No, surely it would be better to delegate, to get someone with less to lose to take the risk.

He added:

4. Ask the gravedigger and/or the young man with a van
   who cuts the cemetery grass to get the chairs.

A quandary. He tried to convince himself that number 1 was the best option. His wife would certainly approve. Anyway, the chairs were almost certainly damaged. Why else would the publican put them in a skip?

But tantalisingly, the skip remained in the car park and, despite his best efforts to concentrate on higher things, if anything his preoccupation with the discarded chairs grew. Whenever he passed the pub he did his best to avert his gaze, but invariably he'd see a flash of yellow out of the corner of his eye.

Then at last, the skip wasn't there any more! The relief, like steam escaping from a pressure cooker, was palpable. He could get on with the rest of his life, no longer haunted by chairs in a skip.

That evening, sipping a G&T and snug in her dressing gown and slippers, his wife enquired about his day.

'Thank you, my dear. As it happens it's been an exceptionally good day. Yes, a very good day indeed. The skip I told you about, the one outside the pub, has gone.'

His wife smiled. 'Ah, I wondered if you'd noticed.'

'I know it sounds foolish,' Father Bill continued, 'indeed it *is* foolish, but it has come as a great relief. I no longer have to fret about whether or not to rescue those chairs.'

The next day Father Bill had occasion to visit the village hall and was astonished to find eight chairs arranged in a neat row with a handwritten note on one of the seats:

Dear Father Bill

Your wife told us you'd had your eye on these chairs. Please accept them with our compliments.

Steve and Mavis from the Red Lion.
PS We've had them cleaned up.

Once again, divine intervention had come to Father Bill's rescue.

The Offer

My name is Rose, short for Rosemary. I'm eighty-seven, in a nursing home and not very well. I get small strokes with no warning. I know when it's happening because my eyes go funny and I feel dizzy. It wears off after a while, but I feel washed out for a couple of days afterwards.

I'm feeling okay today, sitting in my armchair by the window, looking at some photos of myself when I was in my twenties. I've only a few photos from that time, all black and white. Normal people didn't take many photos in those days, not like they do now with selfies and all the rest of it.

I looked pretty good when I was young: an oval face, blue eyes, a trim figure, blonde hair, red lipstick, a bit of eye makeup – I was a smasher, that's what all the boys told me.

I've just shown my photo to the helper who's brought me a cup of tea, a youngster from Poland. I could see she was surprised it was of me. Funny the way young people forget we oldies were all young once. Still, I suppose when I was young I never really bothered to think about old people, and I never thought I'd get old and decrepit myself one day.

Looking at these photos taken in the 1950s brings bad memories. In fact, I'm not sure why I do it. They were all taken by him, so naturally he isn't in any of them. He didn't want his wife to find out. They are mostly of me posing on my own. I threw away all the embarrassing photos long ago, not that I ever had many of those because he kept them for himself.

I can remember exactly what he looked like: rather podgy, spectacles, balding, and with a moustache that looked as if it would tickle. Funny thing is, I can't really remember his voice. Still, it was all a long time ago so perhaps that's not surprising.

He didn't talk to me at all at first. Just ignored me. Or at least I *thought* he did. Later he claimed he'd noticed me on my very first day, but he gave no sign. He was the boss, you see, and I was a junior in the typing pool, only sixteen and fresh out of the 'tech. He was old enough to be my father, smoked cigars and was obviously filthy rich. He wasn't just the boss, he owned the whole company! Every day he parked his black Rover right outside the front door beside a sign that said 'Reserved for the Chairman'.

In a funny sort of way, I suppose what happened was my fault because I got really cheesed off with him ignoring me. I'd got used to blokes fancying me: wolf whistles when I walked down the street, hands all over me when I went out on a date. I didn't expect *him* to fancy me, only to acknowledge my existence.

To start with he barely glanced up when I entered his office to put stuff in his in-tray. Whenever I took dictation, I'd sit there cross-legged, leaning slightly forwards to show a bit of cleavage. But he just gazed out of the window searching for the right words. Then he'd say, 'That's it, Rose. I need those letters typed in time to catch the afternoon post.'

No 'thank you', but at least he knew my name. That was something, I suppose.

Anyway, I got more and more resentful, him ignoring me like that. I started doing things to see if I could get his attention. I'd pretend I hadn't heard something and ask him to repeat it. I'd drop my pen and make a fuss scrabbling around picking it up. I'd sneeze and blow my nose, hoping he might say 'bless you' or ask me if I had a cold. I'd spend ages gathering my things together after taking dictation. Silly little things like that. But none of it worked; he didn't appear to take any notice.

So, I stepped up my campaign. Getting him to notice me became a game. Sometimes I'd stay on after five o'clock, when everyone else had gone, and go into his office without knocking, pretending to be surprised when I found he was still there.

'Oh, sorry, sir. I thought you'd gone home. I only popped in to check your trays.'

'No problem, Rose, just finishing off.'

Sometimes I'd loiter outside the building waiting for him to come out and 'accidentally' appear when he was getting into his car.

'Good night sir. Drive safely.'

'Thanks, Rose. See you tomorrow.'

See me tomorrow! Progress.

I'd been working there for about a year when one evening, after I'd stayed late clearing up, he asked me where I lived. I told him with my parents and that I was saving up to get my own place. He asked if I had any brothers or sisters and I told him no, it was just me. He nodded and said it must be lonely, but I told him I had a boyfriend. After that, every now and again he'd ask me about my boyfriend. What did he do? What did he look like? What sports did he play? What football team did he support? Did we go to the cinema? Stuff like that.

Another year went by. I got promoted and earned a bit more money but my mum became very poorly, skin and bones, in and out of hospital, and eventually she died. I was only eighteen but I'd never been particularly close to her. She didn't really approve of any of my boyfriends. Her death wasn't unexpected, but my dad went to pieces and started drinking heavily.

I took some time off for my mum's funeral. When I went back to work, my boss asked me if I was okay. Did I tell you his name? I always called him sir, but his name was Clive Richardson. Not that it matters, it was all so long ago.

We started to have longer chats after that. He was a busy man, so I was flattered that at last he was showing some interest in me. He was always very polite. He'd enquire about my dad and, in particular, kept asking about my boyfriends. He seemed fascinated. How many did I have? Where did I meet them? Didn't they get jealous? Did I have a favourite? What colour was his hair?

Things steadily got worse at home. My dad lost his job and moped around all day, drinking and feeling sorry for himself. His debts mounted up and he was forced to put our house up for sale. A bit of a wrench. It was only an ordinary semi-detached but I'd lived there all my life. I moved in with one of my boyfriends. He still lived at home with his mum but she objected to us sleeping together. It was very awkward, with lots of unpleasantness and rows, so I started to look for somewhere else to live.

I didn't tell my boss but he noticed I was taking the occasional half-day off and asked me what I was up to. I told him my dad was selling the house and I was looking for a place to rent. That's when he made his offer: he'd set me up in a flat and pay the rent, but I mustn't tell anyone.

I was lost for words, too flustered to ask any questions. I just blurted out that I'd think about it. He said to let him know in the morning, but that I mustn't tell anyone or he'd withdraw the offer.

To be honest, I wasn't sure what to do. It was an amazing offer but what was the catch? Was he setting me up to be his mistress? In all the time I'd worked for him, he'd never attempted to touch me or made any improper suggestions. He'd always seemed more interested in my boyfriends than in me. It was a puzzle, but I decided to accept his offer and see how things turned out. If he turned nasty, I could always move out.

Within a week he had found a place and he took me to see it. The house had recently been divided into self-contained flats. The one he showed me was on the ground floor. It had its own front door that opened straight into a sitting room with a small kitchen area in one corner. A short corridor led to a nice a bedroom with a small bathroom beyond. The flat was empty when I first saw it but he said he'd get it furnished. I was over the moon.

Two weeks later he gave me the keys and said it was ready for me to move in.

The flat looked quite different now that it was furnished. The sitting room had an armchair and a sofa in front of a gas fire. The kitchen was stocked with crockery and cutlery and some saucepans. The bedroom had a double bed with a padded headboard, side tables with lamps, and a dressing table. There was also a three-bar electric fire. A large mirror had been fitted on the wall opposite the bed.

It was luxury. I couldn't believe my luck.

After a few weeks, he started to enquire about boyfriends again. Had I broken up with the last one? When would I get another one? I didn't like to tell him it was none of his business, so I said I was between boyfriends at the moment but there was plenty of talent at the local dance hall.

Not long after that I took a boyfriend back to the flat. His name was Steve. He was amazed to find I had such a nice place and asked me how I could afford to pay the rent. I just smiled and shrugged my shoulders. After drinking some bottles of beer together and mucking about on the sofa, he finished up staying the night.

A couple of days later, I found an envelope tucked away in the top drawer of my bedside table. It had money in it and a brief note.

Rose

Well done! Keep the bedroom lights on next time and the covers off. Don't worry about using the electric fire, I'm paying for it.

The note wasn't signed but I recognised the handwriting.

It felt creepy at first but I got used to it, convincing myself it was a small price to pay for a rent-free flat. I never knew when he was watching. He never said anything but whenever I brought a different boyfriend home, a few days later I'd find he had left an envelope with money in it tucked away in the top right-hand drawer of my dressing table. No message, just money.

A couple of years later he had his accident and it all came to an end. The flat was in his name and the solicitor sorting out his affairs told me I'd have to move out. Anyway, I couldn't have afforded the rent. I moved away and got a new job.

And a new boyfriend.

I've never told anyone about this – well, not until now. If I told my Polish carer, I bet she wouldn't believe it!

Perhaps I shouldn't have mentioned his name. Still, it was a long time ago and I expect anyone who might have been interested is dead by now.

The Professor

The professor's wife loved sweets but the professor didn't really approve. He was worried she might become diabetic. Although she wasn't exactly overweight, she always had some sweets about her person, particularly boiled sweets and jelly beans. He'd catch her rummaging around in her handbag pretending to look for something else and, having located the sweets, surreptitiously popping one into her mouth. Sometimes she offered him one, but not often because she knew he disapproved.

The professor and his wife had been married for forty-seven years and, as their forty-eighth wedding anniversary approached, he decided to go to his wife's favourite sweet shop and buy her a jar of jelly beans. He entered the shop with considerable trepidation, having previously only ever crossed the threshold as her companion. She knew exactly where her favourite sweets were and, without hesitation, would go straight to them as if she had a built-in homing device.

On his own in the sweet shop, the professor felt overwhelmed. Despite being a professor of philosophy with numerous publications to his name and honorary awards from many universities, the sight of so many shelves heaving with row after row of jars containing different coloured sweets discombobulated him. His strong preference was to mull things over, to ponder unhurriedly in his own time, to carefully weigh up the pros and cons of a course of action. He hated situations that called for quick decisions or confronted him with too many choices.

It wasn't that the professor was against choice as such, just *too much* choice that called for too many fine discriminations. How, he asked himself, could his local supermarket display so many subtly different Ryvita biscuits – Dark Rye, Multigrain, Sesame, Pumpkin Seed, Black Pepper, Sweet Onion – when all he wanted were the straightforward, ordinary ones? Suffering from choice overload, he'd invariably decline to make a decision and flee the scene empty handed.

He had the same problem with Netflix. Too many films and too much choice would plunge him into an unwelcome state of dissonance. He'd recently invented a rule that had eased the problem somewhat: he'd only countenance watching films that lasted less than one hundred minutes, preferably less than ninety. Since very few films met this criterion, he'd found that strict adherence to this rule had reduced his choice to manageable proportions.

The sweet shop, stocked from floor to ceiling with brightly coloured sweets, was in gross violation of the professor's preference for limited choices. He stood there, in the familiar grip of indecision, and was about to depart when the young woman behind the counter smiled at him sweetly and said, 'How can I help you?'

The professor, looking desperately around the shelves, replied, 'Jelly beans, where are the jelly beans?'

'You want to buy some jelly beans?'

'Well, yes, but not for me, they are a present for my wife. She loves jelly beans.'

The young woman beamed. 'I'm partial to the odd jelly bean myself. How many would you like?'

For the first time the professor looked at the young woman. She was wearing a bright-blue apron over a green T-shirt. On the bib of the apron, emblazoned across her chest in white letters, were the words *100% happiness guaranteed.* The professor blinked and read the words again. Happiness *guaranteed?* 100%? His mind was racing.

'Excuse me, but where did the slogan on your apron come from? Is that something you dreamt up or is it official?'

'Oh no, it's the company's promise. It's on all our aprons and on the ribbon we use to tie parcels.' She indicated tidy reels of coloured ribbons all saying, in endless repetition, *100% happiness guaranteed.*

'You're *promising* 100% happiness?' asked the professor, staring fixedly at the young woman's bosom.

'Yes,' she said, looking down at her apron. 'No one has ever queried it before.'

'Incredible, quite incredible,' muttered the professor, shaking his head in disbelief. 'I've never before seen such a brazen claim.'

'Well, that's as maybe,' said the young woman, keen to change the subject. 'Did you say you wanted jelly beans? How many? We sell them by weight or you can buy a whole jar.'

'Oh,' said the professor, a touch irritated at being pulled back from his musings, 'it's our wedding anniversary. I'll take a jar.'

When the professor got home, he hid the jar of jelly beans in the bottom drawer of the rolltop desk in his study and sat contemplating the receipt. After a while, he stirred himself and Googled 'Happy Sweets Ltd' and clicked on 'About us'.

There it was again: *100% happiness guaranteed.*

He read: *If you're not 100% happy, we guarantee we will immediately put it right – refunding, replacing or issuing you with a Gift Card as appropriate. We never want you to lose faith in Happy Sweets and we will always go the extra mile to ensure you are happy. All the members of our Customer Care Team are trained and empowered to help. You can always be sure of a prompt, helpful and friendly reply.*

How, he wondered, could a sweet company guarantee happiness? He had always subscribed to John Stuart Mill's belief that happiness was a by-product and that the pursuit of happiness was a fool's errand. He likened happiness to a crab: it always approached you sideways and often when you least expected it.

The professor made an uncharacteristically swift decision: he'd email Happy Sweets Ltd. He clicked on 'Contact Us' and wrote:

Dear Customer Care Team,

I recently bought a jar of jelly beans from your shop in Covent Garden and I was astonished to see that you are guaranteeing 100% happiness. Since the time of Aristotle, philosophers have had much to say about the concept of happiness but, to the best of my knowledge, no one has ever dared to suggest it could be guaranteed, least of all by procuring sweets. Could you please clarify precisely what sort of happiness you are guaranteeing?

I look forward to hearing from you.

Professor Alex Funnell (retired)
PS My wife loves your jelly beans.

Within five minutes the professor received a reply.

Hi Alex,

Thank you for contacting us. Our happiness promise dates from the foundation of Happy Sweets in 1979. We are proud of our products and have no hesitation in guaranteeing the quality of our sweets and, should you order them online, their timely delivery. I hope this provides the clarification you are seeking and look forward to continuing to be the sweet provider of your choice.

Wishing you a happy day!
Felicity, Customer Care Team, Happy Sweets Ltd.

The professor read the email again with increasing incredulity. He considered it inadequate, needlessly flippant and irritatingly cheerful. He made a cup of tea while pondering how best to respond.

Dear Felicity,

Thank you for your reply and good wishes. Unfortunately, you have failed to provide an adequate reply to my previous email. Would you be so kind as to answer the following questions?

1. What precisely is your company's definition of happiness?

2. What do you mean by 100% happiness?

Thank you.
Professor Alex Funnell (retired).

The professor's laptop fell silent. A reply came the next day.

Hi Professor,
Felicity is on sick leave and has passed your email to me. I am Jessica, the supervisor of the Customer Care Team.

May I respectfully suggest that perhaps you are taking our happiness guarantee too literally? It simply means we want our customers to be happy with our sweets and with the service we provide.

Please give me your postal address and I will be happy to send you a complementary jar of sweets. Would you like more jelly beans or a different variety? You can find a full list of our sweets on our website. Just click on 'Our Products' and let me know your choice.

Thank you for your interest in Happy Sweets.
Jessica Browning, Supervisor, Customer Care Team, Happy Sweets Ltd.

The professor was at a loss to know what to do next. Not only had the latest email again failed to provide the information he sought, it invited him to visit a website and choose which sweets he wished to have – the last thing he wanted to do. Anxious to avoid experiencing another bout of choice overload, he decided to send another email.

Dear Jessica,

Please give Felicity my best wishes for a speedy recovery. I hope my email was not in any way a contributory factor to her becoming unwell.

Thank you for offering to send me a complementary jar of sweets, but I remain intrigued by your happiness guarantee. Having read the text of the guarantee again, I venture to suggest it is too all embracing. Indeed, I fear it leaves you open to being sued by anyone who is unhappy for any reason, or, if not actually unhappy, just not happy. Sadly, if one is to believe the latest data on depression and mental illness, this could apply to many millions of people regardless of whether they have purchased any of your sweets.

I think you'd be wise to amend your happiness promise by stipulating that you are not guaranteeing general happiness and wellbeing but limiting your promise specifically to happiness in relation to the quality of your products. I urge you to take remedial action as a matter of urgency.

Professor Alex Funnell (retired).

The next day, the professor received a reply.

Dear Professor Funnell,

Allow me to introduce myself. I am the CEO of Happy Sweets Ltd and your emails have been passed to me by our Customer Care Team.

Firstly, may I say how grateful I am for your intervention. Our 100% happiness strap line was dreamt up by our late founder, Krystian Lewandowski, a refugee from Poland, who had a limited grasp of the subtleties of the English language. The extraordinary thing is that no one has ever queried our happiness promise for more than forty years. On reflection, I can see that, whilst well-intentioned, the promise is too bold and leaves us vulnerable to mischievous legal claims. We are therefore removing the happiness promise from our website and instructing our lawyers to review the wording as a matter of urgency.

Secondly, I understand you recently bought a jar of our jelly beans as a present for your wife. We wish to reimburse you in full for your purchase and, in addition, offer you a lifetime voucher that will permit you and your wife to have sweets from our Covent Garden outlet entirely free of charge. Please send me your postal address and the voucher will reach you by return.

It only remains for me to thank you again for taking the trouble to alert us to what could have become a considerable problem.

Yours sincerely,
Robert McDonald, CEO, Happy Sweets Ltd.

The lifetime voucher duly arrived. The professor retrieved the jar of jelly beans from the bottom drawer of his desk and wrapped it in brown paper, held in place with generous amounts of Sellotape. He put the voucher in an envelope, sealed it and wrote, *Happy Forty-Eighth Wedding Anniversary* on the front. He smiled to himself when he realised he had inadvertently used the happy word.

At breakfast on their wedding anniversary, the professor's wife opened the parcel. She beamed happily at the sight of so many jelly beans and gave the professor a thank-you peck on his forehead. 'That's wonderful, Alex. Jelly beans make me happy.'

The professor suppressed an urge to question the veracity of this claim.

The professor's wife then opened the envelope and read the voucher. 'Free sweets? For *life*? How have you manged that?'

The professor chuckled. 'It's a long story, my dear, but I can assure you Happy Sweets will be very pleased, perhaps even relieved, to know you're happy.'

The Risk Taker

I expect you are curious to know how I finished up in jail when I've always been such an upstanding citizen?

Well, unlikely though it might seem, it all started when I was a choirboy. I was only eleven and I found the sermons seriously, excruciatingly, boring. Anyway, to pass the time I used to sketch the people sitting in the choir stalls opposite. They were the *decani* and we were the *cantoris*. I only slipped some Latin in to impress you. After all, opportunities to impress people are in short supply aren't they? I find throwing in a bit of Latin every now and again often does the trick. Not something corny that everyone knows like *tempus fugit* or *carpe diem*, but something more obscure like the Latin name for daisies, *bellis perennis*, or for forget-me-nots, *myosotis*. Impressed, eh? Thought you would be.

Anyway, as I was saying, I was in *cantoris* on the south side of the chancel, sitting immediately opposite the other half of the choir on the north side. A bit like the setup in the House of Commons, except it wasn't really a 'them and us' situation.

However, the *decani* were sitting ducks, as it were, all in rows just asking to be drawn.

I'd have sketched the preacher droning on, but the pulpit was on our side of the church so sketching him would have been a bit obvious. I'd have had to crane my neck, and even then I'd only have been able to glimpse the back of his head. Mind you, he had big sticky-out ears so a sketch from behind would have been a laugh.

I used to sketch the grownups in the second row of *decani*: the basses, tenors and altos. They were real characters, with wrinkles, moustaches, receding hair lines, specs – things that made them interesting. Mr James, the bass, was fat with a round face and double chin that wobbled when he sang, whereas Mr Butler, the tenor, was like a scarecrow with an Adam's apple that bobbed up and down. I drew them over and over again during weeks of boring sermons, and the caricatures gradually became more unforgiving. Fortunately they never knew I was drawing them or, if they did, they didn't let on.

I used to hide a piece of paper inside a copy of *The English Hymnal*, making sure I kept it below the height of the stall. The only give away was when the boys sitting either side of me glanced at what I was doing and sniggered. Fortunately that didn't happen often because they'd be engrossed in reading something or other during the sermon. No one seemed to listen to the preacher, not even the congregation, as far as I could tell, and they were there *voluntarily*! It always struck me as rather weird to choose to perch on uncomfortable church pew when you could be outside enjoying yourself. Joining the choir had been my parents' idea. They thought it would do me good, but I was out of there fast once my voice started to break.

At secondary school I did caricatures of all my teachers: the Latin teacher with his big domed forehead; the science teacher with his bulbous nose; the chinless maths teacher; the headmaster peering over his half-glasses. Even though it was so long ago, I can still visualise them now and I could probably still get a good likeness just from memory.

I only came to grief once when the Latin teacher found a particularly unflattering drawing of himself tucked inside an exercise book that I'd handed in for marking. I'd forgotten it was there. He was livid and sent me, clutching the offending sketch, to the headmaster. I think the headmaster thought the sketch was rather good because I could see he was suppressing a smile. He confiscated my sketch and gave me a week's worth of one-hour detentions during which I had to write the sentence 'I must not draw during Latin lessons' over and over again. A bit pointless, really.

Anyway, that's how it all began and I've been a clandestine sketcher of people ever since. The secret is to hide your sketch book inside a newspaper or a book, to look really hard at your victim while they are preoccupied with something else, and to concentrate on memorising just a small bit of them – the shape of their head, for example, or their nose or their eyes. Then look down and commit that part to paper, look up again and memorise the next bit, and so on. Up and down, up and down, like a pigeon pecking at breadcrumbs. If they should happen to glance your way, stop dead and gaze around innocently, or put your head down and pretend to read. Oh, and wearing dark glasses helps put them off the scent.

It's been fun seeing if I could complete a half-decent sketch without being spotted. For years I worked in the visual-aids department at the Civil Service Staff College producing endless transparencies for overhead projectors and, after they went out of fashion, for PowerPoint. All tame stuff, not much scope for creativity, but at least it was a job. When the college closed, I was offered a redundancy package and off I went, liberated. After a few months of loafing around not doing much, I started to sketch people again and got a cheap thrill out of seeing if I could avoid detection. A bit like being a voyeur!

I've taken some risks just for the hell of it. I found pubs were a good place to sketch. You get some real characters slowly getting sozzled in pubs. It's a bit tricky if they rumble what you're up to but, as long as you stay sober, you can scarper before they get you. I once tried sketching in the public gallery of the House of Commons just because I knew it wasn't allowed. Unfortunately I was soon spotted. My sketchbook was confiscated and I was escorted out of the building by two policemen.

I also experimented with drawing nudists on Studland Beach. Some wonderful wobbly shapes – a free life-drawing class! I managed a couple of hours without being detected but eventually a big guy spotted me drawing his buxom girlfriend and roared, 'Pervert!' I ran for it. My fault really, I shouldn't have spent so long drawing her tattoos.

Despite these setbacks, or more probably *because of them*, I got more and more hooked on seeing if I could get away with sketching people in dodgy situations. I know it sounds daft, but it gave me an adrenalin rush, became something of an obsession.

My downfall came after reading an article about courtroom artists. It explained how they aren't allowed to do any sketching in the courtroom itself. The artist has to memorise whoever they want to sketch, usually the defendant, and dash outside and do the drawing from memory in the corridor or the press room. This intrigued me and I started to wonder whether I could do sketches in court without being apprehended.

I started by experimenting in the local magistrates' court but that was too easy because no one took any notice. I think they assumed I was a reporter from the local rag. So I decided to try the Old Bailey. I booked a tour first so that I could suss the place out and check the security arrangements. You have to go through the usual airport-type security and of course you can't take in mobile phones or any large bags. I worked out that if I had a very small sketch pad in my inside pocket it would probably get through, and an ordinary biro would have to suffice.

They publish a list of the cases that are going to be heard each day and I chose a nice juicy murder case, a lorry driver accused of killing his wife. I got into the courtroom okay and sat in a corner of the public gallery. It wasn't too crowded so I didn't have anyone sitting particularly near to me. I sketched the defendant, a big burly fellow with a furrowed brow and a crew-cut, then I moved on to sketching members of the jury and a couple of witnesses.

Then – well, I got too cocky and decided to sketch the judge with his wig and all his gear. He had a big beak of a nose and very bushy eyebrows. I don't know how he knew he was being drawn, he must have sensed it somehow, telepathy maybe. Anyway, he suddenly looked straight at me and halted the proceedings. I was pounced on and frogmarched out of the court. I was caught red handed, all very embarrassing. Subsequently I was charged with contempt of court and given a six-month jail sentence. Reminded me of being put into detention all those years ago.

So here I am in Wandsworth. Mind you, it could be worse, a lot worse. Word has got around that I'm the artist who had the audacity to do a sneaky drawing of the Beak. There are some tough characters in here, but they're lining up for me to do portraits for their girlfriends. The tattoos, as ever, will be a challenge.

The Shadow

He prided himself on leading an orderly life. Stephen was a successful businessman who ran his own publishing company. The publications were all of the self-help 'you can do it if you really want to' pop-psychology genre. There were paperbacks about healthy eating, healthy exercising, healthy breathing, healthy relaxation, healthy sex and healthy brains. The books sold well and Stephen's company flourished.

Remarkably, Stephen, in his mid-fifties, even practised what he preached. He rose early and grinned at himself in the mirror whilst mouthing 'new day, new opportunities'. After warming up with a series of slow lunges and squats, he went for a brisk thirty-minute walk, followed by twenty minutes of meditation. Each day he took 1000 milligrams of fish-oil concentrate, ate porridge for breakfast, and was careful to have at least five portions of fruit and vegetables and drink three litres of water. Stephen came as close to being a paragon of virtue as mere mortals ever can.

One day Stephen went to a Business in the Community conference. One of the speakers, using the results of a recent survey to show how careers in business were regarded as second best to those in the professions, spoke persuasively about the need to forge stronger links between education and business. He concluded by suggesting that every business should 'adopt' a local school and explore ways to help teachers and students to understand and better appreciate the world of work.

Stephen came away from the conference fired up and determined to play his part. He contacted the head teacher of the local comprehensive and offered his services. He rejected an invitation to come into the school a few times a week to hear some of the junior children reading aloud, explaining that he was a busy man with a business to run. Could he perhaps offer work experience to sixth formers?

So it came to pass that Oliver, a seventeen-year-old lad, arrived one Monday morning, looking decidedly bolshie, with a rucksack slung over one shoulder.

In the week immediately prior to Oliver's arrival, Stephen had encountered some unwelcome resistance from his management team. They had made it clear, not for the first time, that they were understaffed and couldn't possibly waste time explaining things to a naive student. Oliver, they insisted, was Stephen's idea and he'd have to take full responsibility.

So, disappointed but undaunted, Stephen had spent time conscientiously planning how to give Oliver a sufficiently meaningful experience. He had read and reread the briefing sheet that the school's careers teacher had provided and drawn up a plan for the week that contained ample variety. It included a tour of the office, an initial question-and-answer session about the company and its products, and a couple of mini-projects scrutinising the business plan and some of the company's marketing literature.

But the bulk of the week was to be spent shadowing Stephen as he went about his business, including visiting a large trade exhibition in Birmingham, and accompanying him on some customer visits. Stephen had even persuaded his management team to agree, somewhat grudgingly, to allow Oliver to sit in and observe the weekly staff meeting.

Stephen was confident that he'd planned a model week that would be an admirable advertisement for the much-maligned world of work. Over the weekend, feeling virtuous, he even told his wife that he was toying with the idea of offering work experience for sixth formers on a regular basis. She quietly suggested that he'd best survive the week with Oliver before making any long-term commitments.

'Welcome to Healthy Publications, Oliver,' Stephen beamed, overlooking the fact that Oliver was twenty minutes late.

'It's Ollie, not Oliver.'

'Oh, sorry. The school told me you were Oliver.'

'Yeah, but everyone calls me Ollie.'

'Right. Anyway, we've got a busy schedule lined up for you but, before I run you through the programme, let me ask you what you're hoping to get out of your week with us.'

'How d'you mean?'

'Well, today is Monday. What are you expecting to have gained by five o'clock on Friday?'

'I'll have to leave by three on Friday. It's football practice.'

'That could be tricky. We'll be on our way back from Birmingham on Friday afternoon.'

'I can't miss football practice, we've got a big game on Saturday.'

'I see. I suppose I could re-jig the programme,' Stephen conceded reluctantly. 'We could go up to Birmingham on Thursday instead of Friday.'

Not, he thought, a promising start. The boy seemed ill-prepared and aimless. Never mind; Stephen was confident that the various activities he'd planned for the week would help Oliver, or rather Ollie, to see the importance of being reliable and purposeful.

Stephen produced his 'Ten Commandments', a document he always shared with new starters. He gave Ollie a copy and expanded at length on the merits of each point. It read:

Do these things and you'll exceed my expectations.

1. *If you aren't clear about something, ask. Questions are always welcome.*

2. *If you are unhappy about something, always say so. Don't let things fester.*

3. *If you see something that needs doing, just do it (it's easier to ask for forgiveness than for permission!).*

4. *Experiment with different ways of doing things in order to find a way that works best.*

5. *When you make a mistake (<u>when</u>, not if!), say sorry and learn from it.*

6. *If you can see a way to improve something, go ahead and suggest it.*

7. *If you aren't sure what other people think about something you've done, ask for feedback.*

8. *If something you've done is criticised, remember it is what you did that attracted the criticism – not you as a person.*

9. *Choose to be purposeful and positive rather than aimless and negative. The choice is yours!*

10. *Use work as an opportunity to grow and develop your talents.*

'Cool,' said Ollie. Seemingly underwhelmed, he stuffed the page into the back pocket of his jeans.

On Monday afternoon a key member of staff, the woman who looked after the accounts, unexpectedly gave in her notice. She told Stephen she'd had a row with the office manager who had refused to allow her to go on vacation even though she had already booked a holiday and paid a non-refundable deposit. Apparently hostilities between her and the office manager had been building up over a long period and she had reached the end of her tether.

Stephen, appalled to discover strife in his team of which he was unaware, immediately brought the two women together in a well-meaning attempted to negotiate a peace deal. This rapidly descended into a slanging match with both women screaming obscenities at each other, and ended abruptly when the accountant quit without serving out her notice and the office manager, in floods of tears, locked herself in the toilet.

'Sorry about all that,' Stephen said to Ollie. 'The day turned out to be rather more exciting than I'd planned. Never mind, we'll get back on track tomorrow.'

'Cool,' said Ollie, his thumbs busy texting something to someone on his Smartphone.

On Tuesday, just as Stephen had started to brief Ollie on the company's marketing strategy, news reached the office that a lorry on its way to deliver a large print run of some of their best-selling publications had collided with a tanker on the motorway and burst into flames. Apparently both drivers had escaped unharmed from their cabs, but the fire had been ferocious and both lorries had burnt out, melting a large area of tarmac and closing the motorway for the rest of the day. This left the company's stock levels disastrously low and everyone had to abandon their normal duties and spend time on the phones apologising to customers and reimbursing them for orders that could no longer be fulfilled.

'Well, Ollie,' said Stephen at the end of a fraught day on the phones, 'I hope you can see how we have to stay nimble, on our toes, ready to adapt to unexpected events. Life in business is never boring, that's for sure.'

'No worries,' Ollie said. 'Pity we didn't get to see the fire.'

On Wednesday, just as Stephen had started to brief Ollie on the five-year rolling business plan, a VAT inspector arrived unannounced, demanding to be provided with a quiet office and all the financial documentation for the previous year. Stephen, caught on the hop, asked if the inspector could perhaps return on another day since the person who looked after the accounts had left suddenly and not yet been replaced. The inspector would not budge, however. He insisted that the whole idea of an on-the-spot check was that it should be on the spot, thus preventing the possibility of any 'er, um, window dressing'. The inspector, clearly not a fan of winning friends and influencing people, spent the day ensconced in Stephen's office, painstakingly going through the accounts and querying everything he suspected might be dodgy. Once he'd discovered that £135 was owed in unpaid VAT he became more affable, professing himself delighted with his day's work.

'Well, Ollie,' said Stephen, having spent the day at the beck and call of the inspector, 'yet another example of our little plan bumping up against reality! Never mind, tomorrow's another day and I'm sure you'll find our visit to the NEC illuminating. It's an hour and a half's drive up to Birmingham so we need to leave promptly at 8.30am.'

'Cool,' said Ollie, pulling on his coat.

That evening Stephen, chatting with his wife over a glass of non-alcoholic wine, admitted that he wasn't looking forward to Ollie accompanying him to the exhibition centre. 'He's morose and monosyllabic, not exactly good company,' he sighed. '"Cool" is all he ever seems to say.'

The next morning Ollie sauntered in ten minutes late, not that it really mattered because Stephen was on the phone apologising to a disgruntled author who had not received her royalty payment.

'She's always grumbling,' Stephen explained as they fastened their seat belts. 'You'd never guess she'd written a best seller on healthy gratitude!'

The drive to Birmingham took longer than expected because of a slow crawl past miles of road works on the motorway. As they crept along, Stephen waxed lyrical about the joys of being in the publishing business, radiating faith in how self-help books transformed people's lives. Ollie, as usual, seemed unfazed.

For the last leg of the journey, horrified to discover that Ollie had never heard of Leonard Cohen, Stephen put on his favourite CD. He paused it every now and again to explain the meaning of some of the more obscure lyrics. Ollie showed no sign of sharing Stephen's appreciation of Leonard Cohen's undoubted genius.

Eventually they arrived at the NEC later than planned and parked the car. They set off on a brisk walk to the exhibition centre but had only gone a few yards when Stephen grimaced, dropped his briefcase and clutched his chest. He staggered, attempting to steady himself by grabbing the wing mirror of a nearby Range Rover, but his legs buckled and he collapsed onto the tarmac like a faulty deckchair.

Ollie immediately swung into action. He phoned 999 on his mobile, asked for an ambulance and put his phone on speaker. He loosened Stephen's tie, tilted back his head and checked whether he was breathing.

'We're at the NEC, Car Park 2, row K. My boss has stopped breathing. I think it's a cardiac arrest. I'm starting CPR now.'

'An ambulance has been dispatched. What's your name?'

'It's Ollie.'

'Are you alone with the casualty? Do you know what to do?'

'I've done first aid. Got my Duke of Edinburgh's award. We've practised on dummies.'

'Good lad. It's your boss, you say?'

'Well, sort of. I'm shadowing him for the week.'

'How old is he?'

'Could be my dad. In his fifties, I guess.'

'The ambulance is about five minutes away.'

Ollie, continuing with vigorous, rhythmic chest compressions, managed to say, 'Thanks. That's cool.'

The ambulance duly arrived and the paramedics took over.

'Well done, mate. A brilliant job. You deserve a medal.'

Stephen's heart was restarted with a defibrillator and he was stretchered into the ambulance. It drove away at speed with its blue lights flashing. Ollie brushed himself down, picked up Stephen's briefcase and walked to the station to catch a train home.

On Friday evening, after football practice, Ollie received a phone call from Stephen's wife.

'Is that Ollie?'

'Yep.'

'I'm phoning from my husband's bedside. The paramedics said you saved his life. How can we ever thank you?'

'No worries,' said Ollie.

The Silver

Every Christmas Eve my father polished the silver. It was an annual ritual that he appeared to relish, though it was hard to be certain since my father was an undemonstrative man.

He always followed the same routine. First he would prepare by covering the kitchen table with newspaper and then donning an apron and a pair of rubber gloves. Next he'd retrieve the tureens, platters and candelabra one by one from the depths of the dining-room sideboard, place them on a tray and carry them to the kitchen to begin his sacred task.

Once he'd polished all the pieces, he'd carefully arrange them in a display on top of the sideboard. They were never used; they just sat there catching the light. Then, before going to bed on Twelfth Night, my father put all the silver back in the cupboard where it would languish until its next appearance on Christmas Eve the following year.

We lived in a modest Victorian semi. Apart from the silver, there was nothing about it that was in the least ostentatious. When I was a toddler I took the silver's annual outing for granted, standing on tiptoe and giggling at my distorted reflection. Once my mother found me at full stretch trying to lift a piece down. Panic-stricken, she shouted, 'Don't touch that! Your father will be furious.'

I was an only child – my mother was thirty-nine and my father forty-three when I was born – and my father clearly resented the fact that I was a girl. Throughout my childhood he was always short-tempered, leaving me in no doubt that I was an unwelcome complication in his life. He was never a tactile man, no hugs or kisses, always spurning any displays of emotion.

After my mother died and he was left to fend for himself, I sometimes plucked up the courage to ask him how he was feeling. It seemed impertinent to ask something so intrusively personal, with its implication that he might not be coping. His stock reply was always the same: 'Mustn't grumble.'

So I have never been close to my father though he has slowly mellowed over the years and gradually become more tolerant and less critical of me.

It was only when I became a teenager, experimenting with red lipstick and wearing skirts my father considered too short, that I became really curious about the mysterious silver that appeared like clockwork every Christmas, was never used and, it seemed, could only be handled by my father. It slowly dawned on me that not only was the silver off limits, it was incongruous and totally out of keeping with everything else in our utilitarian home.

Whenever I questioned my father about the silver he snapped, 'None of your business, young lady.' It was as if I were asking something outrageously risqué. My mother was a little more forthcoming, telling me in hushed tones as if sharing an intimate secret that she believed the silver was a family heirloom and had once belonged to my paternal grandfather.

My father has always walked with a limp. My mother once told me that he'd been a young officer in Singapore when the Japanese were advancing down through the Malayan jungle. She said he'd been wounded in the fierce fighting before the surrender in 1942.

Intrigued, I asked him about his wartime exploits. What had happened to him? Had he been a prisoner of war, or had he evaded capture and, if so, how? But he was never forthcoming, shrugging his shoulders dismissively. 'A long time ago. Never you mind.' The only information he once grudgingly imparted was that he had stayed on in the army after the war, rising to the rank of major and leaving in 1956 before meeting and marrying my mother.

My father has been a widower for eight years now, and during the last two he has become increasingly confused and frail. It's been sad to see. He was always proud and fiercely independent, but gradually the problems escalated beyond control when he started to have accidents: cutting himself with a saw; scalding his hand with boiling water while making a cup of tea, and having one fall after another.

Grudgingly, he eventually agreed to go into a care home but, he insisted, only to give himself time to recuperate and regain his strength. In the meantime, I am keeping the house ticking over because he still remains obstinately convinced that he'll be able to return to independent living.

Once incarcerated in the bosom of the nursing home, however, his energy deserted him. He has become inactive, he just sits and gazes out of the window. When I make my weekly visits he often says nothing; if he does speak, it is to complain that the staff bully him. He claims that they delight in placing his cups of tea out of his reach and that they make him take showers that are much too hot and chuckle when he protests.

Gradually he has become thinner and weaker. A few months ago, he took to his bed. Sides have now been fitted, like a cot, to prevent him falling out.

With no normal chit-chat possible, and feeling desperately bored, I have taken to reading aloud to him from whatever book is near to hand. He never gives any indication of appreciating this, but neither does it seem to irritate him. Often I think he dozes off. When it's time for me to leave, he'll stir himself just enough to whisper accusingly, 'Don't leave me like this!' Ignoring my guilty feelings, I tiptoe out anyway, tell the nurses I'm off and step outside with a sigh of relief, relishing the fresh air and freedom.

After my dutiful visits, I usually call in at my father's house to check that all is well and continue sorting through his belongings. It is not an easy task; after my mother died, my father let things go. He became an avid reader, never bothering to tidy up or do any routine maintenance. I don't remember him reading books when my mother was alive but, once he was alone, he bought books from the nearby Oxfam shop for a pound or two and he'd sit for hours engrossed in one after another. As a consequence, discarded books clutter the whole house, heaped in ungainly piles on every available surface.

I intended to pack the books into cardboard boxes and return them to the charity shop, but I have discovered they have all been defaced. My father has scrupulously underlined words and passages in every single one, often with a red biro, and written numerous comments in the margins and on the inside covers: *Too slow, skipped lots of it; Gripping stuff, read it twice; Crap; Definitely a woman's book; A bugger's muddle, should never have been published; Hard going, print's too small.*

Safe in the knowledge that I had the house to myself, one of the first things I did was to take a good look at the forbidden silver. As I lifted each piece out of the sideboard, it felt as if I were doing something outrageously wicked, like breaking into a reliquary and fondling the bones of a saint. Absurdly, I imagined my father suddenly entering the room and catching me red-handed.

I was surprised to discover that many of the pieces were damaged. I hadn't noticed this before; on its annual outings, my father had clearly arranged the silver so that the damage faced the wall. I wondered what trauma had caused the silver to get bent and dented and what, even in its damaged state, it might be worth. Had my father ever had it valued? Was it insured? Should I get it insured? Uncertain about the best way forward, I carefully wrapped the pieces in newspaper, returned them to the cupboard and closed the doors.

Most of the books in my father's collection are adventure stories – he was particularly fond of books by Wilbur Smith – but there are also books about WW2, and some about the war in the Far East. Conspicuous amongst the paperbacks is a solitary hardback: *The Defence and Fall of Singapore, 1940–1942* by Brian P. Farrell.

I flicked through it, looking at the passages my father had underlined and reading various comments he'd written in the margins. The chapter describing the fall of Singapore and the ignominious surrender to the Japanese was particularly well-thumbed, with whole paragraphs underlined.

On the inside flyleaf my father, in his neat but pinched handwriting, had written:

1SRRA, B Mati, Xmas '50

Found myself back in the old officers' mess. Apparently, the Japs had used it as a comfort station.

Regiment in the process of disbanding. Handing over to the Gurkhas.

My mission: to locate the regimental silver. Drunk when we dumped it in the jungle, so only a vague idea of where to search. Bonkers, but had to pretend to take it seriously.

Fortunately, the colonel knew it was a longshot. Never let on about our 50–50 arrangement.

Intrigued, I decided to have another look at the silver. I unwrapped each piece in turn, examining them carefully under the light cast by my father's Anglepoise lamp. On some I could make out an engraving – 1SRRA – nearly erased by my father's rigorous polishing over many Christmas Eves. What might 1SRRA mean? Might it be some sort of obscure silver mark?

I looked online and was astonished to be taken to a website about Sentosa, a resort in Singapore. There I read that Sentosa, now a small pleasure island, had previously been a British garrison called Blakang Mati, home to the 1st Singapore Regiment, Royal Artillery, and that, after fierce fighting in 1942, the island had been overrun by the Japanese.

One paragraph in particular jumped out at me. It read:

There's an intriguing story among soldiers who served on the island after the Second World War. In the last days before the British surrendered to the Japanese, British officers, fleeing the Officer's Mess, hid the regimental silver to prevent it from being captured by the Japanese. Some of the silver was recovered in Malaysia, while the rest might still be buried somewhere on the island.

When next I visited my father, I opted to read him the chapter in Farrell's book about the Japanese entering Singapore. My father lay in his cot, his eyes closed as usual, giving no indication of whether he was listening or not. Undaunted, I finished the chapter, turned to the flyleaf and read aloud the note my father had written.

I put the book aside, leaving the words 'never let on about our 50–50 arrangement' hanging in the air.

After a pause, my father stirred and did something I'd hardly ever seen him do: he smiled.

The Success Predictor

He felt exhilarated, confident he'd got it made. Like a trainspotter witnessing a lovingly restored steam engine emerging from its shed, he knew perfection when he saw it.

Most people would have thought that breaking free from the institute, with its job-for-life security and badge of respectability, was a rash move. But George Silvester, not yet 30, was never given to self-doubt.

'Are you quite sure you want to do this?' the principal asked, having just read George's letter of resignation. 'I could tear it up and we could forget the whole thing.'

'Thanks for the offer, but I'm quite sure I'm doing the right thing.' George squinted back through his thick lenses, gently stroking his goatee beard – a mannerism he had cultivated when he wanted to look studious and worldly-wise.

'Well, if you insist. I must admit,' the principal chuckled, 'life will be a lot easier without you continually whingeing about the way we do things. But we'll be sorry to lose you.'

George smirked at the back-handed compliment. 'Thanks, but I've done my research, got all the ducks in a row and

173

secured a lucrative contract. I'm definitely onto a winner!'

'Well, good luck to you,' the principal said insincerely, 'one has to admire your pluck.'

George had always been a loner. A slight figure with an unruly mop of hair, at school he had hated any sporting activities, preferring to read a book or play chess, twitching with glee as he plotted his opponent's downfall. He was academically gifted, worked hard and emerged from university with a BSc, first class, in Mathematics and Statistics. Remarkably, he'd never been picked on nor bullied. People tended to leave him to his own devices.

George's decision to quit his job at the institute and become self-employed could be traced back to his initial obsession with doodles. He couldn't help but notice how often his students whiled away the time by doodling on their notepads whilst ostensibly listening to his lectures. George was an uninspiring lecturer. He considered lecturing to be a chore that took him away from his precious research projects, but his contract required him to deliver a few hours of lectures each month so, grudgingly, he obliged.

George saw that his students' doodles fell into two broad categories: those with predominantly straight lines, and those with predominately curved lines. At first he thought it might be a gender thing – women inclined to ovals and circles and men to squares and triangles – but he quickly realised this was too simplistic.

Might there be, George wondered, a correlation between the type of doodle and academic performance? Perhaps students who doodled using straight lines outperformed those who were predisposed to curves? Or vice versa? Or might the type of doodle be something to do with differing personalities? For example, straight for extroverted, curved for introverted? Or vice versa?

He researched 'significance of doodles' and found more than sixteen million entries on the web, but everything he read seemed to be pure conjecture, home-spun stuff with no scientific basis.

Intrigued, he decided to conduct an experiment. He'd deliver an even more boring lecture than usual and conclude by inviting his students to hand in whatever doodles they had produced. He'd stress that participation was entirely voluntary and promise to share the results of his analysis with those who were interested.

All went according to plan, apart from some students dozing off rather than doodling and two Chinese girls who, giggling deferentially, claimed they hadn't doodled because they'd found the lecture so enthralling! George received twenty-eight pages of doodles from a class of forty-five, more than enough for a preliminary analysis.

He set to work, but his attempts to sort the doodles into meaningful categories and correlate them with academic performance proved fruitless. One evening, after easily winning a game of chess against Dave, a fellow statistician at the institute, he shared his frustration. 'I'm sure doodles signify something, but exactly what eludes me right now.'

'You're on a hiding to nothing with something as daft as doodles,' Dave laughed. 'Even Freud gave up on them.'

'Yes, but surely they can't just be random? They must have *some* significance.'

'Maybe, but no one has sussed it out and it's not for want

of trying. Your only hope is to reduce the variables.'

'No doubt, but it would be a nonsense to dictate what people should doodle. Surely free expression is of the essence?'

'Ah well, I'll leave you to sort out that conundrum but, if I were you, I'd turn my attention to something more worthwhile.' Dave stooped to tie up his shoe lace. 'How about why the lace on my right shoe undoes itself, never my left?'

'Very funny,' said George. 'A double bow would sort that out.'

'That would undoubtedly solve the problem but fail to explain why it happens.'

'If you don't mind, I'll stick with doodles.'

'Well, don't say I didn't warn you,' said Dave, putting on his anorak and stuffing his things into a small rucksack.

George mulled over the conversation. Reduce the variables. He knew that was the key, but how?

Then he had his brainwave, his light-bulb moment.

It took a further two years of experimentation and thorough testing of the reliability and validity of his discovery before George was ready to launch his website. He had been canny enough not to divulge his formula to anyone, neither was it written down anywhere. It was just in his head.

George designed his own website: SuccessPredictor.org. It was unashamedly boastful, claiming to predict with 99.9% accuracy whether an aspiring entrepreneur would be successful. There were no upfront fees to pay, only a contract to sign giving George a 10% stake in the entrepreneur's business venture. George was happy to wait for his rewards, confident that in the fullness of time the accuracy of his success predictor would make him a very wealthy man.

But absolutely nothing happened: there were very few visitors to his website and certainly no takers.

'You need some enthusiastic endorsements on social media from the likes of Richard Branson and James Dyson,' Dave suggested, after suffering another humiliating defeat at chess. 'How about getting a dragon from *Dragons' Den* on board?'

George spurned television and had never seen the programme, but he watched some videos of the dragons putting would-be entrepreneurs through their paces and quickly realised they were missing a trick: they spent too much time scrutinising the viability of the business proposal and not enough assessing whether the proposer was a winner.

George knew, knew for sure, that they should be using his success predictor.

He contacted the BBC and, with his usual conceit, more or less said 'here I am, come and get me'. He was invited to a meeting with one of the programme's researchers, a young, earnest-looking woman called Rachel. They sat in a corner of the cafeteria.

'So,' said Rachel, consulting a document on her clipboard, 'you say you are able to predict the likelihood of a venture being successful?'

'Yes, absolutely. Not just the likelihood, the *certainty*.' George stroked his beard and gave Rachel one of his self-satisfied smiles.

'But how can you possibly do that? If we're to go forward with this, we'll need irrefutable evidence and cast-iron proof that it works.'

'I'm afraid I can't divulge exactly how it works – that must remain a commercial secret. But I'm happy to provide you with all the statistical data backing up my claim.'

'Well,' said Rachel, standing up abruptly to signify the meeting was over. 'Send us the data and we'll take it from there.'

'Sure,' said George, 'but don't leave it too long. Lots of other people are showing a keen interest,' he lied. 'I'm giving you first refusal.'

'Send us the data and we'll take it from there,' Rachel repeated, seemingly unmoved at the prospect of competitors scrambling to secure rights to the success predictor. She escorted George to the lift without saying another word.

George duly submitted his data and, after a few weeks, was pleased to receive an invitation to another meeting. This time he was ushered into a small side room where, after a fifteen-minute wait, he was joined by two middle-aged men. There was no sign of Rachel.

'Thanks for coming in, Mr Silvester,' said the man with greying hair. 'I'm Harry, one of the producers of *Dragons' Den*, and this is Stuart from the BBC's legal department. We have looked at your research findings and found them very interesting. We've taken the liberty of running them past a statistician and he has confirmed that your methodology appears to be sound.'

'Just as I expected,' George smirked.

'However,' Harry continued, 'I'm afraid we cannot proceed unless you are prepared to share your formula with us. We require total transparency. No transparency, no deal – it's as simple as that.'

'But,' said George, stroking his goatee beard, 'if I told you exactly how my success predictor works I'd have no bargaining power. You could copy my discovery.'

'Mr Silvester, I can assure you that's not the way we do

business,' said Stuart, the lawyer, quietly, as if aghast at the possibility of any skulduggery. 'You must appreciate that we have contracts with thousands of creative people and our reputation depends on respecting their intellectual property. In fact, we are prepared to offer you a generous upfront fee, but it is conditional upon you being entirely open with us. It's a matter of trust.'

''A fee?' George gazed at them through his thick lenses, keeping a straight face and concealing any signs of excitement.

'Yes,' said Harry. 'Our offer is set out in this document, which you are welcome to take away and peruse at your leisure.' He slid an envelope across the table. 'In summary, we are offering you a one-off payment of £10,000 in return for the exclusive use of your success predictor, and thereafter we'll pay you a consultancy fee of £20,000 per programme. As you know, we make ten programmes per season, so I'll leave you to work out the maths.' He smiled at George. 'We very much hope you'll decide to work with us and look forward to a beneficial collaboration.'

'Thank you,' said George. 'I felt sure you'd see the merits of using the success predictor.'

'And,' Harry added, 'as you are probably aware, versions of *Dragons' Den* are produced in approximately thirty other countries around the world. Whilst we can't make any promises, it is highly likely that your success predictor will be of interest to at least some of them.'

As soon as George had left the building and turned the first corner, he punched the air and let out a whoop of joy. Passers-by looked at him askance and gave him a wide berth. On the train journey home he calmed himself and read through the contract a couple of times. He gazed out of the carriage window. Might it be worth seeing if they would stump up more? But surely a contract worth £200,000 per annum, plus the possibility of more from foreign versions of the programme, was more than adequate? Especially for such a simple discovery.

George duly signed the contract, together with a legally binding clause forbidding him from disclosing anything to anybody about his association with the programme. It was to be a clandestine collaboration. Not wishing to appear too eager, he waited for a few days before posting it, together with details of how the success predictor worked, by recorded delivery. By return came a countersigned copy of the contract and a cheque for £10,000.

Then nothing happened: no calls, no involvement in the programme. Nothing.

George emailed Rachel, only to receive a curt, out-of-office reply. He phoned and a secretary, claiming to know nothing about his contract, promised that someone would get in touch.

But they didn't. He phoned again, asking to be put through to Harry or Stuart, but was told they were abroad attending a conference and would be in touch upon their return. George waited anxiously but still nothing happened.

One evening, feeling fraught after Dave had beaten him at chess, a rare reversal of the usual outcome, George decided, despite the non-disclosure agreement, to tell him about the arrangement. 'Do you remember you suggested I should get in touch with the *Dragons' Den* people?'

'Anything come of it?'

'Yes. I'm not supposed to tell anybody, but they gave me a contract.'

'Great! So why are you looking so glum?'

'Well, I can't understand it.' George shook his head. 'It seemed such a promising deal but nothing has happened and they aren't answering my calls.'

'And you've agreed they can have exclusive use?'

'Yep, that's right.'

'For how long?'

'In perpetuity.'

'What? You clown, they've got you stitched up!'

'How come?'

'My guess is you'll never hear from them again.'

'But why? I don't get it.'

'Because they've realised your success predictor would wreck the programme.'

'Wreck the programme? How come?'

'Think about it. The entertainment value of *Dragons' Den* thrives on uncertainty. Being able to predict the success of a venture would remove the need for the dragons to take a gamble when deciding whether or not to invest their time and money.'

'So what can I do?'

'Absolutely nothing, mate. They've decided to gag you, simple as that. You'd better get to work and dream up something else.'

In a rare display of emotion, George slammed his fist on the table. Chess pieces scattered as if taking fright. 'Bloody hell! And I was sure I was on to a winner.'

'Dare I ask,' said Dave, 'if you took your success predictor yourself?'

'How could I? It would be like marking my own homework.

I invented the bloody thing. I was the only person in the world who knew how it worked.'

'And how does it work?'

'Simple. You ask someone to draw a road disappearing into distant hills. Successful entrepreneurs draw roads with straighter lines than those that are destined to fail. Meandering roads are a sure sign of failure.'

Dave laughed. 'You're kidding! And they gave you ten grand for that? Cheer up, mate, you should definitely clock that up as a triumph.'

George looked unconvinced.

The Switch

D r Noel Palmer, a retired academic, eighty-five years of age, slightly hard of hearing and renowned for being polite and mild tempered, had banked with the same bank for more than fifty years. He was unadventurous when it came to banking, just as he was with most things, and had never been brave enough to venture into online banking. He was content with setting up direct debits for regular payments and writing cheques for everything else. He found it comforting to have a branch he could visit – though, he calculated, he hadn't had occasion to do that for well over twelve months.

One day Noel read an article in his newspaper about inertia and how organisations took advantage of loyal customers who failed to shop around. He resolved there and then to be uncharacteristicaly adventurous and switch his current account to another bank. Perhaps after that he would change his electricity provider, his car insurer, his home insurance, his investment manager, his internet provider...

Yes, from now on he would embrace change! It would be exciting, a welcome antidote to his humdrum, repetitive life.

Why, he fantasised, he might even move house, stop wearing ties, grow a beard, join the local bowling club, change his pet tortoise. The possibilities were endless!

Intoxicated by his own recklessness, Noel visited the local branch of Pretty Bank (chosen for no other reason than he liked the name and because they were offering a reward of £125 if you opened an account with them). Feeling emboldened, he stood in a queue for a short time humming quietly to himself. Once he got to the counter, he told the young woman behind the glass that he wished to switch his current account from Ugg Bank.

'Excellent, and congratulations on choosing Pretty Bank. Rest assured that we'll look after everything. We've done this for hundreds of esteemed customers who, like you, have wisely decided to switch banks. You'll not regret it.'

Her name badge said *Sharon*, and beneath it a comforting slogan said: *We value your custom.* She gave him a broad smile; her teeth were suspiciously even and, he thought, much too white.

'Thank you for your reassurances, dear lady. I must admit to having succumbed to inertia and stayed with Ugg Bank for as long as I can remember. I'm finding the prospect of making the change quite exhilarating.'

'You'll definitely not regret it, sir. Nothing ventured, nothing gained!' Sharon flashed him another gleaming smile.

'I hope so. Can you confirm the procedure?'

'Of course. You need to provide us with proof of identity such as your passport or driving licence, and proof of address – a recent utility bill will suffice. We contact your bank request-ing them to supply us with a list of your standing orders and direct debits. We then set up the appropriate mandates and notify you when the transfers have been done. After that, you authorise Ugg Bank to close your account and transfer the balance to us. You sit back and let us do all the work. It's all quite straightforward.'

'Splendid, splendid! Straightforward – that's the reassurance I need.'

'We pride ourselves on under-promising and over-delivering, sir. I can assure you that you are safe in our hands.' Another smile.

That afternoon, Noel returned to the bank and provided Sharon with all the documents she required.

An uneventful week passed. Noel pottered around contentedly, humming absentmindedly to himself whilst doing this and that: some gardening; completing the cryptic crossword in *The Times*: continuing his research into the life and times of Neville Chamberlain, and cataloguing his collection of political cartoons.

From time to time he wondered when he'd be told that it was safe to close his account with Ugg Bank, but he was content to wait, confident that things were progressing satisfactorily as Sharon had promised.

Then Noel received an unexpected phone call. 'Pretty Bank here, Dr Palmer. Just a courtesy call. I'm a supervisor in the quality assurance team. It's my job to check that we are following the correct procedures. Could you please confirm your Ugg Bank account details?'

'Why? I've already given you everything you need to proceed with the switch.'

'I know, Dr Palmer, and I apologise if this seems repetitious, but we pride ourselves on our rigorous attention to detail.'

Noel sighed but, having a high regard for quality and orderly procedures, he cooperated and provided all the information the caller requested. 'Thanks for your patience, Dr Palmer. Everything seems to be proceeding satisfactorily and we'll be in touch in the next few days to confirm that your new account is up and running.'

Another humdrum week passed but then a letter arrived from Noel's local authority saying that his monthly direct debit had been cancelled and that his council tax payments were in arrears. This was unsettling. Not being accustomed to falling behind with any payments, he phoned Pretty Bank; he would have gone to the branch in person except that it was pouring with rain. He listened patiently to part of the second movement of Schubert's 'Trout Quintet', interrupted with occasional explanations about how busy they were, how his call was important to them and that it might be recorded for training purposes.

Eventually his call was answered. 'Thank you for waiting. My name is Marcus. How may I help you?'

'I was hoping to speak to Sharon. Is she there?'

'She's not in today but I'm sure I can help you.'

'I do hope so. I have received a puzzling note from the town hall alerting me to the fact that this month's council tax hasn't been paid. You assured me that you'd look after everything and that switching my account from Ugg Bank would be trouble free.'

'Right,' said Marcus. 'I just need to take you through some security questions.' Noel obliged, going through the familiar routine of providing his name, his address, his place of birth, his mother's maiden name, the name of his first pet and the account number he'd been given.

Marcus put him on hold and the 'Trout Quintet' resumed.

'Thank you for waiting, Dr Palmer. I have checked that your direct debit for the council tax was included on the list sent to us by Ugg Bank and I'm glad to say that everything is in order.'

'Well, obviously everything isn't in order. Why hasn't the council tax been paid?'

'I'm afraid you'll have to ask Ugg Bank that question. I can assure you that we are following our normal procedures and everything is in hand. May I help you with anything else?'

Feeling increasingly exasperated, Noel phoned Ugg Bank. After listening to reggae music, interrupted by the usual apologies for the lines being busy, for being held in a queue and assurances that his call was valued, a voice said, 'Thank you for waiting. My name is Diana. How may I help you?'

'I'm in the process of moving my account to Pretty Bank, but it seems that the direct debit payment for the council tax has gone awry. I was told to contact you to find out what's gone wrong.'

'I just need to take you through some security questions,' Diana replied.

Noel sighed but obliged, reminding himself to be patient as he went through the familiar rigmarole.

After a pause, Diana said, 'I can confirm that your account has been closed and the balance transferred.'

'The account has been closed? But why? I didn't give my authorisation.'

'Yes, it's definitely been closed and your debit card has been cancelled. Is there anything else I can do for you, Dr Palmer?'

'Wait a minute! This isn't supposed to happen. I was told that I would be informed when the switch had been completed and when it was safe to close my account with you.'

'I can assure you we have followed our normal procedures and that the account has been closed.'

Feeling uncharacteristically indignant, Noel raised his voice. 'This is outrageous! I have not authorised you to close my account. You must reinstate it immediately.'

'I'm afraid that isn't possible. Once an account has been closed, it can't be opened again for two years.'

'This is unacceptable, completely unacceptable! I wish to speak to your manager.'

Diana put him on hold, but not before saying 'bear with me', an expression that had always jarred. Noel hung on feeling increasingly stressed, listening to inappropriately cheerful music and concentrating on his breathing – in, to a slow count of four and out, to a slow count of six – a calming technique he'd adopted after it was recommended on a recent Radio 4 programme.

'Dr Palmer,' said an unfamiliar voice. 'I believe you've asked speak to me about closing your account?'

'Yes, that's correct. My account shouldn't have been closed without my authorisation and I want it opened again.'

'But, Dr Palmer, if you recall, you phoned last week to confirm that you wanted us to transfer the balance and close the account. We were merely carrying out your instructions.'

'I phoned?' said Noel, completely nonplussed.

'Yes, there's no doubt about it. It's all here in our records. You passed security and provided us with everything we needed to transfer of funds.'

The truth slowly dawned. Noel, feeling weak at the knees, sank down onto the nearest chair. He'd read numerous stories in his newspaper about elderly folk like him being conned, and now it had apparently happened to him. He felt panicky and embarrassed about being taken in so easily.

He stirred himself, adjusted his hearing aids, put on his mac, found his umbrella and, avoiding the puddles, marched to Pretty Bank.

'Is Sharon here?' he asked the woman at the counter, someone he hadn't seen before.

'No, we don't have a Sharon. How can I help you?'

'Well you *did* have a Sharon a couple of weeks ago. Where is she?'

'I'm not really at liberty to say, but I believe she has left the bank. Pastures new and all that.'

'Left the bank? Wasn't that rather sudden? Never mind. Could I ask you to check whether my new account has been opened?'

The woman took Noel's account details and consulted her screen. 'Yes,' she nodded, 'I can confirm that it's up and running.'

'And the current balance?'

'One-hundred and twenty-five pounds.'

'No transfers from Ugg Bank?'

'No, just £125 at present.'

Noel nodded and, even though he could anticipate the answer to his next question, he asked it nonetheless. 'Tell me, when switching accounts, is it normal to get a call from your quality assurance people?'

'That's a new one on me. The switching service is a perfectly straightforward process. We've done it for thousands of customers. It only remains for you to tell your old bank to transfer the balance and we're in business.'

Noel sighed. 'Regrettably that will not be possible. It seems that £9,362.53 has been spirited away to I know not where.'

Crestfallen, Noel trudged back through the rain, telling himself he'd been a gullible old fool. Embracing change, he reflected, had been a costly exercise. From now on he'd content himself with embracing the status quo.

Humming a dirge to himself, he stopped abruptly when he reached his front door and realised that, in his haste to get to Pretty Bank, he'd forgotten his keys.

To Whom It May Concern

I hadn't seen her for more than thirty years – until last night, that is. I'm afraid her sudden reappearance after such a long absence feels – well, ominous. Hence this note. Just in case.

I didn't believe she'd left me at first. I carried on with my life, keeping busy, trying to get back on an even keel, expecting her to turn up sooner or later. And now she has. She was always secretive, never one to explain herself. Easy come, easy go. No goodbyes, never said where she was going. Just vanished for thirty years.

It's difficult to know where to start. I was only a teenager, lacking self-confidence and flattered by her attentions. I've no idea why she chose me. You'd think she'd have had something better to do, but she persisted. She seemed like an older sister, just a tease, all innocent enough to start with.

It took some time for me to rumble her because the risks she got me to take often worked out okay, like being a gambler on a winning streak. You have to admire the way she did it, lulling me into her confidence and only gradually raising the stakes.

She never told me her name, but once it dawned on me

that she was the one orchestrating my mishaps, I nicknamed her Miss Hap. Seemed appropriate. She never commented, just smiled and winked. She often did that. I used to find it a real come-on.

I'm monitoring my oxygen levels at the moment. I've been feeling breathless lately and my doctor told me to get this little gadget. You clip it on your middle finger and it gives you a reading. Between ninety-five and a hundred is fine, but sometimes mine drops below that. I'm a bit breathless and my pulse rate is higher than usual, too.

When Miss Hap made her surprise appearance last night, she spent ages looking over my shoulder at my readings. She didn't comment on them, just nodded and gave me one of those tantalising winks as if to say 'I know something you don't know'.

I was still at school when I first became aware of her. She was the one who got me smoking fags behind the cricket pavilion on summer evenings after prep and then, when winter came, in the loft above the dorm. It was quite cosy up there, a small group of us huddled round a solitary flickering candle, puffing away, the tips of our fags glowing in the gloom.

We were all in chapel singing hymns when the fire broke out on a Sunday morning. The roof collapsed into our dormitory and we had to sleep in the sanatorium for a year while a new wing was built.

It was her fault that I got glandular fever, which mucked up my mock A Levels. I'd never have plucked up the courage to ask the Latin teacher's daughter for a kiss without Miss Hap daring me to do it. And all those passionate necking sessions that followed (as it happens, behind the cricket pavilion) wouldn't have happened. I'd have just moped around lusting from afar.

Without her egging me on, there's no way I'd have agreed to visit the red-light district on that school trip to Amsterdam. Getting caught by that teacher (what the hell was he doing there anyway?) and being expelled was her fault, really. Well, I say it was her fault but, to be honest, attributing blame isn't entirely straightforward. You see, she only ever *suggested* things, leaving me free to decide whether or not to take up her suggestion.

Mind you, she was always very persuasive. She had a way of making me feel invincible, that I could do anything I put my mind to. Skiing is a good example. I remember standing at the top of a black run at the end of a long day's skiing thinking shall I or shan't I? Ice had started to form and the run was steep and narrow. The friends I was with thought it was too dodgy and were preparing to turn back.

Then she appeared, smiling as usual. 'Go on, Stephen, what are you waiting for?' she said in her soft, purring voice. 'You know you can do it. Don't let your friends talk you out of it. Go on, you show them.'

So with one push on my poles, I launched myself. My fall was dramatic; I parted company with my skis almost immediately and sped down the slope on my front, arms outstretched like a demented bobsledder. I was rescued hours later after my friends raised the alarm. Two broken arms and a dislocated shoulder.

I'm still breathless and my oxygen levels have dropped below ninety-five. I've phoned for an ambulance but they say they're very busy. Could take three hours.

She loved it when I got my pilot's licence. I'd be flying solo on a clear day over Oxfordshire, little dinky fields far below, when she'd appear and suggest trying something more adventurous — flying in some tight circles, looping the loop a few times, pulling the throttle back and putting the plane into a spin. The thing is, she was right; it *was* a bit boring flying along straight and level, and it *would* be more fun to try some manoeuvres. How was I to know that the plane would be written off, and that I'd be lucky enough to get the canopy open and escape with my parachute? Of course there was no way I could explain my moment of madness to the satisfaction of the Board of Inquiry, so my licence was withdrawn.

That was typical of her. She'd appear, urge me to do something risky then scarper and leave me to face the consequences. She was never around when I came a cropper, which is fair enough, I suppose, since she never actually *made* me do anything. Just put the idea into my head and, like Japanese knotweed, once it was there it was hard to get rid of.

Not everything she suggested was life threatening. Some were merely embarrassing, like the time she hid the notice saying 'women only' on that sauna, or the time she got me trapped in the office lift with my boss's secretary, or the time at that conference when she assured me my microphone was switched off when I went for a pee.

But things gradually escalated. Getting stuck for the night on that deserted island off the Croatian coast wasn't funny. I bloody nearly died of hypothermia before they realised I was missing and came back for me. My motor-bike accident wouldn't have happened if she hadn't been riding pillion and urging me to go faster. And the way she encouraged me to invest all that money in my friend's dodgy business venture — disastrous. Cost me my marriage and my house.

Then she buggered off, leaving me until last night with a leg full of nuts and bolts, living alone in rented accommodation.

The paramedics are here now, a man and a woman. They're very friendly but they look as if they've come from outer space, all dressed up in PPE. They've done various tests and say I need to go to hospital. The woman has just nipped out to get a stretcher. She gave me a wink as she left.

About the Author

D r Peter Honey worked as an occupational psychologist, specialising in interpersonal skills and lifelong learning. He is the author of many management books and self-assessment questionnaires, including the widely used Honey & Mumford Learning Styles Questionnaire. He is married and lives in Windsor.

Email: peterhoney1@btinternet.com
Website: www.peterhoney.org